IMRE KERTÉSZ

KADDISH
FOR AN UNBORN CHILD

Translated from the Hungarian by TIM WILKINSON

A NOTE ABOUT THE AUTHOR

Imre Kertész, who was born in 1929 and imprisoned in Buchenwald as a youth, worked as a journalist and playwright before publishing *Fatelessness*, his first novel, in 1975. He is the author of *Looking for a Clue, Detective Story, The Failure, The Union Jack, Kaddish for an Unborn Child*, and *Galley-Slave's Journal*. He was awarded the Nobel Prize for Literature in 2002. He lives in Budapest and Berlin.

A NOTE ABOUT THE TRANSLATOR

Born in England in 1947, Tim Wilkinson first began translating from Hungarian after living and working in Budapest during the early 1970s. He has translated a number of works of history, including Éva Balázs's *Hungary and the Habsburgs 1765–1800*, Domokos Kosáry's *Hungary and International Politics in 1848–1849*, and Viktor Karády's *The Jews of Europe in the Modern Era*, as well as literary works by many contemporary Hungarian prose writers.

Books by IMRE KERTÉSZ

Fatelessness

Liquidation

Looking for a Clue

Detective Story

The Failure

The Union Jack

Kaddish for an Unborn Child

Galley-Slave's Journal

KADDISH

FOR AN UNBORN CHILD

IMRE KERTÉSZ

Translated from the Hungarian by Tim Wilkinson

VINTAGE INTERNATIONAL
Vintage Books
A Division of Random House, Inc.
New York

FIRST VINTAGE INTERNATIONAL EDITION, OCTOBER 2004

Cataloging-in-Publication Data
for *Kaddish for an Unborn Child* is on file at the Library of Congress.

ISBN 1-4000-7862-8

Book design by Mia Risberg

www.vintagebooks.com

Printed in the United States of America
10 9 8 7 6 5 4 3 2 1

"... streicht dunkler die Geigen dann steigt ihr
als Rauch in die Luft
dann habt ihr ein Grab in den Wolken
da liegt man nicht eng"

Celan: *Todesfuge*

"... more darkly now stroke your strings then as smoke
you will rise into air
then a grave you will have in the clouds
there one lies unconfined"

Celan: *Death Fugue*[1]

---

[1]Translation by Michael Hamburger (*Selected Poems of Paul Celan*, Anvil Press Poetry, 1995; Penguin Books, 1996)

KADDISH

FOR AN UNBORN CHILD

"No!" I said instantly and at once, without hesitating and, virtually, instinctively since it has become quite natural by now that our instincts should act contrary to our instincts, that our counterinstincts, so to say, should act instead of, indeed as, our instincts—I'm joking, if this can be regarded as a joking matter; that is, if one can regard the naked, miserable truth as a joking matter, is what I tell the philosopher approaching me, now that both he and I have come to a halt in the beech wood, beech coppice, or whatever they are called, stunted and almost audibly wheezing from disease, perhaps from consumption; I must confess to being a dunce about trees, I can recognize only pine trees instantly, on account of their needles—oh yes, and plane trees as well, because I like them, and even nowadays, even by my counterinstincts, I still recognize what I like intuitively, even if not with that same chest-thumping, gut-wrenching, knee-jerking, galvanizing, inspired, so to say, flash of recognition as when I recognize things I detest. "I don't know why it is that every time everything is different in every respect with me, or perhaps if I do know, it's simpler that I know without knowing it. That would spare me a lot of explanations. But, it would seem, there is no getting around explanations, we are constantly explaining and excusing ourselves; life itself, that inexplicable complex of being and feeling, demands explanations of us, those around us demand explanations, and in the end we ourselves demand explanations of ourselves, until in the end we succeed in annihilating everything around us, ourselves included, or in other words explain ourselves to death," I explain to the philosopher with that compulsion to speak, to me so abhorrent and yet irrepressible, that always grips me when I have nothing to say for myself—and that, I fear, has roots in common with the stiff tips that I hand out in brasseries and taxis, or bribing, etc. official or semiofficial personages, along with my exaggerated politeness, a politeness exaggerated to the point of self-denial, as if I were continually apologizing for my existence, for this existence. For heaven's sake! I had simply set off for a walk in the woods (even if it is only this meager oak wood) in the fresh air (even if the air is somewhat putrid) to blow the cobwebs away (let us put it that way since it sounds good, as long as we don't look too closely at the meanings of words, because if we do look, then the words have no meaning at all, do they? since I don't have any cobwebs that need blowing away, quite the contrary, I am exquisitely sensitive to drafts); I am (was) spending my time here, fleetingly (and I will not digress here on the digressions that this word offers), in the lap of this mediocre mid-Hungarian hill range, in a creative writers' retreat—one might call it a holiday home, though it also does for a workplace (for I am always working, being driven to this not just by the need to make a living, but because if I were not working *I would be existing*, and if I were existing I don't know what that would drive me to, and it is better not to know, although my bones, my guts have their hunches, to be sure, since the reason I work incessantly is that as long as I keep working, I am, whereas if I didn't work, who knows whether I would be or not; so I take it seriously, and I have to take it seriously because a deadly serious association is sustained between my sustenance and my work, that is perfectly obvious); so anyway, in a house where I had gained the right of admittance into the illustrious society of intellectuals of my ilk, whose paths for that very reason I can in no way avoid crossing, for all my soundless lying low in my room—the secret of my hiding place betrayed at most by the muted tapping of my typewriter—and for all my scurrying about on tiptoe in the corridors, one has to have meals, yet then table companions surround me with their relentless presence, and one has to take strolls, yet, smack in the middle of the woods, who should I find coming the other way, in his very own stocky and incongruous self, in his brown-and-beige-checked cap and his loose-fitting raglan overcoat, with the narrow slits of his whey-colored eyes and his big, soft, kneaded and already risen dough face, but Dr. Obláth, the philosopher. That is his regular civilian occupation, as attested, incidentally, by the relevant entry in his identity card—to wit, that Dr. Obláth is a philosopher just like Immanuel Kant or Baruch Spinoza or Heraclitus of Ephesus, just as I myself am a writer and literary translator, and the only reason I do not paint myself in an even more ridiculous light compared with the giants who can be marshaled behind the banner of my craft, giants who were genuine writers and, in some cases, genuine literary translators, is because I look ridiculous enough as it is having this as my profession and because my activities as a literary translator nevertheless invest my efforts at keeping myself occupied with some semblance of objectivity and, possibly, in some people's eyes—above all, in the eyes of the authorities and, albeit for different reasons, of course, in my own eyes too—of a verifiable profession.

"No!" something had bellowed and howled inside me, instantly and at once, when my wife (though as it happens long since not my wife) first made mention of it—of you—and my whimpering abated only gradually, yes, actually only after the passage of many long years, into a gloomy weltschmerz, like Wotan's raging fury during the renowned farewell scene, until a question assumed ever more definite form within me, emerging as it were from the mist-shrouded figurations of stifled string voices, slowly and malignantly, like an insidious illness, and you are that question; or to be more precise, I am, but an I rendered questionable by you; or to be even more precise (and Dr. Obláth, too, broadly agrees with this): *my existence viewed as the potentiality of your being*, or in other words, me as a murderer, if one wishes to take precision to the extreme, to the point of absurdity, and albeit at the cost of a certain amount of self-torment, since, thank God, it's too late now, now it'll always be too late; that is permissible too, you are not, whereas I can be assured of being in complete safety, having ruined everything, smashed everything to bits, with that "no," above all my ill-starred, short-lived marriage, I tell (told) Dr. Obláth, doctor of philosophy, with a dispassion that life may never have been able to inculcate in me but which I have nevertheless by now become quite practiced at practicing should it be absolutely necessary. And it was necessary on this occasion because the philosopher was approaching me in contemplative mood, as I immediately discerned from the slight sideways tilt of his head, on which was flatly perched his rakish peaked-cap, as if he were an oncoming comic highwayman who had already knocked back a few glasses and was now deliberating whether to rap me on the head or make do with some ransom money. But of course (and I was about to say: sadly) Obláth was not deliberating that at all; philosophers do not commonly deliberate about highwaymanship, or if they do happen to, then it manifests itself to them in the form of a weighty philosophical question, and they leave the dirty work to the professionals, for, after all, one has seen that sort of thing before, though it was sheer whimsy and all but an aspersion for me to allow such an association with Dr. Obláth, of all people, to cross my mind, for I know nothing about his past, nor will he recount it, it is to be hoped. No, but he did surprise me with a no less indiscreet question, rather as if a highwayman were to inquire how much money I have in my pocket, for he began to pry into my family circumstances, though, to be fair, only after having first led up to that by informing me about his own, as a down payment, so to say, on the premise, so to say, that if I were allowed to find out everything about him, despite my being not in the slightest bit interested, he would thereby earn the right to my . . . but I shall break off this exegesis as I sense that the letters and words are carrying me away, and carrying me away in the wrong direction at that, in the direction of a moralizing paranoia, a state in which, sadly, I catch myself all too often these days and the reasons for which are all too obvious to me (loneliness, isolation, voluntary exile), not that those reasons worry me since they are of my own making, after all—so to say, the first few scoops of the spade towards the much, much deeper trench that I still have to dig out, clod by clod, from one end to the other, for there to be something to swallow me up (though maybe I am not digging in the ground but rather in the air because there one is unconfined)—since all Dr. Obláth did was ask an innocent question as to whether I had a child; though certainly, with a philosopher's rude candor, which is to say tactlessly and in any case at the worst possible moment, but then, how was he to have known that his question would, undeniably, somewhat upset me. Or that I would then reply to the question with an overwhelming compulsion to speak that sprang from my exaggerated sense of politeness, a politeness exaggerated to the point of self-denial, repellent to me from first to last even as I was speaking, despite which I nevertheless recounted that:

"No!" I had said instantly and at once, without hesitation and, so to say, instinctively since it has become quite natural by now that our instincts act contrary to our instincts, that our counterinstincts, so to say, act instead of, indeed as, our instincts; yes, I was seeking to get back at Dr. Obláth—Dr. Obláth, doctor of philosophy, that is to say for all that idiotic blather, for my own voluntary and in no way justifiable (though I had plenty of justifications for it, a few of which I have already spelled out above, to the best of my recall) degradation in portraying him there, slap-bang in the middle of the emaciated beech wood (or linden grove, for all it matters), the way that I portrayed him, though the peaked-cap, the loose-fitting raglan overcoat, as well as the whey-colored eyes and the big, soft face like lumps of kneaded and risen dough, I still maintain, do indeed, accord fully with reality. It is just that it could all have been described otherwise, in a more balanced fashion, more considerately, perhaps even—and this is saying something—*with affection*; but, I fear, the only way I can describe anything now is with a pen dipped in sarcasm, derisively, perhaps even a touch humorously (it's not my place to judge that), yet also in certain respects lamely, as if someone were constantly jerking back my pen when it is poised to set down certain words, so that in the end my hand writes other words in their stead, words that will simply never round out into an affectionate portrait, perhaps simply *because, I fear, there is no affection* in me, but then—for heaven's sake!—for whom might I feel affection; and why? Yet Dr. Obláth spoke endearingly enough, at least enough for me to record in final (I almost said fatal) form several of his more piquant observations, since they aroused my attention. The fact that he was childless, he said, that he had no one apart from an aging wife who was struggling with the problems of aging, if I understood him right, since the philosopher formulated it more opaquely or, one could also say, more discreetly than that, trusting me to understand what I wish to understand, and even though I did not have wish to, I did of course understand all the same. That this matter of his childlessness, Dr. Obláth continued, had actually struck him only recently, but then very often, indeed this was precisely what he had been pondering just now on the woodland path and, lo and behold, he could not forbear to speak about it, presumably because he too was aging and, as a result, certain possibilities—for instance, the possibility of still having a child—were slowly no longer possible for him, indeed were impossible, and that in fact he had only begun to think much about this quite recently, and more specifically, he said, thinking of it "as a missed opportunity." At this point Dr. Obláth halted on the path, for in the meantime we had set off again, two social beings, two men conversing on the forest litter, two sad blots on a landscape painter's canvas, two blots which in their essences shattered a natural harmony that has probably never existed, only I don't remember whether it was I who joined step with Obláth to accompany him or he who joined step with me, but then one is not going to make this a matter of prestige: yes, naturally it was I who joined step with Obláth, most probably in order to shake him off because that way I would be able to turn back at a later point of my own choosing; so anyway, at this point Dr. Obláth came to a halt on the pathway and with a single melancholy gesture stiffened his doughy or even, here and there, puffily exuberant countenance, for he threw back his head, together with its impertinent, rakish cap, to fix his gaze on a tree branch opposite as if on a pitiful, ragged yet, even in its castoffness, still serviceable item of clothing. And while we stood there in this way, mutely, I in Obláth's and Obláth in the tree's axis of attraction, I was assailed by the feeling that I was about to become party to a presumably confidential utterance by the philosopher; and that is indeed what happened when Dr. Obláth finally spoke, and he said that in saying that he felt what had happened—or rather what had not happened—was a missed opportunity he was not thinking of continuity, that somewhat abstract and yet, let's be honest, basically satisfying solace of knowing he had fulfilled—or rather, and that was precisely the point, not fulfilled—his personal and suprapersonal business on this earth, that is, the business, over and above sustaining his existence, of the prolonged and propagated perpetuation and survival of that existence, and thereby of himself, in descendants, which (beyond sustaining one's existence) is, one might say, man's transcendental albeit highly practical duty in life, so as not to feel incomplete, superfluous and, ultimately, impotent; nor was he even thinking of the impending prospect of an old age without support, no, but in truth he feared something else: "emotional sclerosis," as he put it, those were his exact words, meanwhile setting off again along the path, ostensibly heading towards our base, the holiday home, but in reality, as I now knew, towards emotional sclerosis. And I stepped to join him as a faithful companion on this journey of his, duly disconcerted by his disconcerting words though not sharing his fear so much—a fear which, I fear (or rather, to be more accurate, I trust, indeed am sure), is merely momentary and sacred only insofar as it is to be dipped in eternity, as in some font of consecrated water so to speak, because when it eventually comes to pass we shall no longer fear it, no longer even remember that this was what we had once feared, since by then it will have overwhelmed us and we shall be sitting up to our necks in it, it will belong to us and we to it. Because this too is just a hoe's scratch towards the trench, the burial pit that I am digging in the air (because there I shall be able to lie down in comfort), and perhaps that is why, as I say (though I don't say it to the philosopher, just to myself), there is no need to fear emotional sclerosis, one should accept it, if not positively welcome it, like a helping hand extended towards us which, for all that it is undoubtedly helping us towards the trench, is still helping nonetheless; because, Mr. Kappus, *the world is not against us . . . if dangers are at hand, we must try to love them*; but then, I interject (though I do not address this to the philosopher, nor even to Mr. Kappus, the lucky dog to have got so many letters from Rainer Maria Rilke, I just say it to myself) that I am already at the point where *I love these dangers to the exclusion of all else*, though I suppose that is not quite right either, it too carries a false note that I perpetually pick out, just like an orchestral conductor who immediately detects from the tutti if, let us say, the cor anglais tootles a note a semitone sharp on account, let us say, of a misprint that has crept into the score. And I perpetually pick out this sour note, not just within me but also around me, within my more immediate and my broader, what I might call cosmic surrounds, like here, in this lap of shifty Nature, within the surrounds of the sickly oaks (or beeches), the stinking brook and the mucky-hued canopy glimmering through the consumptive foliage, where I, my dear Mr. Kappus, never feel an intimation of any "thought of being a creator, of procreating, of making"—a thought that, wouldn't you agree, *is nothing without its continuous great confirmation and realization in the world, nothing without the thousandfold concordance from things and animals . . .* Yes, because for all that they have put a dampener on us or jaded our spirits (to say no more about it than that), surreptitiously, if we pay quiet and close attention to the circulation of our blood and our alarming dreams, surreptitiously—and only in this do I sense a thousandfold concordance which rings out from everything and everybody—we still, always and unwaveringly, wish to live, this lethargically, this dispiritedly, this sickly, yes, even like this and even if we are unaware of even that much and unable to live even that much . . . For that very reason, and also in order to avoid becoming bogged down in this sentimental mood, in which, as in almost everything, by the way, or at least everything in which *I* too play a part, I yet again clearly heard the sour note of the cor anglais, I posed him a question that very much pertained to his professional domain, a question that though philosophical was perhaps not the slightest bit sophisticated, as to Why this is the way it is, all this decrepitude? Where and when had we finally "got rid of our rights"? Why is it no longer possible to know so inexorably and so definitively what we know? and so on and so forth, as if I didn't know what I know, but driven by my irrepressible compulsion to speak, by some dread, some *horror vacui*; and on Dr. Obláth's face there now resettled the countenance of a professional philosopher and professional intellectual, middle-aged, of medium build, middling means, middling talents and middling prospects professing middling views on a mediocre mid-Hungarian hill range, and the wrinkles of his cynical, happy smile completely engulfed the slits of his eyes. His voice too immediately recovered its objectivity, even objectivism, that well-oiled, habitually hair-splitting and in fact self-assured voice, which had merely faltered momentarily just beforehand at the threatening proximity of real-life things; and so we strolled homewards, two, in point of fact, well-dressed, well-fed, well-preserved, middle-aged, mediocre intellectuals professing middling views, two survivors (each of us in his own different way), two still living, two half-dead individuals, and we discussed, quite superfluously, the sorts of things that can still be discussed between two intellectuals. We discussed, peaceably and desultorily, why it is not possible to be; how the very sustenance of life is, in point of fact, sheer bad manners since, in a more elevated sense and looked at from a more elevated perspective, it ought not to be permissible to be, simply by virtue of events and the continual recurrence of events, let that much suffice, that is reason enough; not to speak of the fact that more erudite minds already proscribed being from being long, long ago. Another thing that was brought up—I cannot recall everything, of course, for hundreds upon hundreds of similar conversations buzzed or rather echoed hollowly in a conversation that had come about as a result of pure confusion and accident, in the way that *in one creative thought a thousand forgotten nights of love revive, filling it with sublimity and exaltation*—I cannot, in truth, recollect everything, but I believe another thing that was brought up was: Is it not possible that the entire seemingly unknowing effort of being that is directed towards being is by no means a sign of some impartial naïveté, which would be an exaggeration and, in point of fact, impossible, but, on the contrary, a symptom that it can continue only this way, unknowingly, if it must continue at all costs. And only if survival is successful, and of course (Dr. Obláth), it can only succeed on a *more elevated plane*, although (duet) not even the faintest signs point to this, to be frank quite the opposite, namely, a descent into unknowingness shows itself to be the case . . . Furthermore, that knowing unknowingness and the syndromes of schizophrenia obviously . . . And yet furthermore, this means that the experiencing (I) and reification (Dr. Obláth) of the state of the world to which every state of the world tends, in the absence of faith, culture and other official devices, is nowadays only a disaster . . . And so we tootled on, tootling the sour-toned cor anglais as on the crowns of the motionless, torpid trees there settled a hazy blue twilight mist, tucked away deep within which, like a dense nucleus, lay the more solid mass of the holiday home, where a laid supper table awaited, a presentiment of soon-to-be-rattling cutlery, clinking glasses, a swelling susurrus of conversation, and out of this stark fact came a plaintive sigh of the sour-toned cor anglais; nor can I pretend to myself that I did not, after all, turn back in order to shake Dr. Obláth off: spellbound and as a result of the emptiness concealed by my compulsion to speak and the bad conscience (disgust) that I felt on account of this emptiness, who knows why, but undoubtedly on account of this emptiness, I stayed with him to the very end in order not to hear, not to see and not to have to speak about what I ought to speak—indeed who knows?—perhaps even write about. Yes, and the night bestowed its punishment—or was it a reward?—for all this, bringing a turn in the weather, a sudden windstorm, claps of thunder and huge strokes of balefully flickering lightning that plowed right across the entire sky then decayed as zigzag hieroglyphics and dry, laconic, clearly—(at least for me clearly)—legible letters, each one a

"No!" that I had said, because it had become quite natural by then for my instincts to act contrary to my instincts, for my counterinstincts, so to say, to act instead of, indeed as, my instincts.

"No!" something within me bellowed, howled, instantly and at once, and my whimpering abated only gradually, after the passage of many long years, into a sort of quiet but obsessive pain until, slowly and malignantly, like an insidious illness, a question assumed ever more definite form within me: Would you be a brown-eyed little girl, with the pale specks of your freckles scattered around your tiny nose? Or else a headstrong boy, your eyes bright and hard as greyish-blue pebbles?—yes, contemplating my life as the potentiality of your existence. And that day, the whole night through, I contemplated nothing but this question, now by the blinding flashes of lightning, now in the darkness with dazzled eyes which, in the capricious intervals between the ragings in the atmosphere, seemed to be seeing this question flicker across the walls, so I must regard the sentences that I am writing down now, on this sheet of paper, as if I had written them down that night, although that night I experienced them rather than wrote them down, experienced them, which is to say was riven by sundry pains, most notably those of memories (I also had a half bottle of cognac), and I jotted down on the pages of one of the notebooks, exercise books or writing pads that I always have with me at best just a few muddled words that I was hard put to reconstruct afterwards, and even then didn't understand, then later on I forgot the whole thing, and it was only after many years had passed that the night stirred into life within me once more, and again years had to pass until I can attempt to write down now what I would have written down that night, had I been writing, and were a single night, anyway, not too short, far too short, for me to have been able to write down what I would have written down. But then, how would I have been able to write, for that night was just the start, probably not the very first but at any rate one of the first steps on the long, long, who knows how lengthy path towards true clear-sightedness, or in other words, towards knowingly known self-liquidation, an initial scraping towards the grave bed which I am making for myself—there can be no doubt about it now—in the clouds. And this question—contemplating my life as the potentiality of your existence—proves a good guide, yes, as if, clutching me with your tiny, fragile hand, you were leading me, dragging me behind you along this path, which in the end can lead nowhere, or at most only to a totally futile and totally irrevocable self-recognition, and a path down which one may (why the "may"? even "must" does not begin to express it) set off only by removing the barriers and impediments that loom along it; first of all by removing, I would go so far as to say radically uprooting, my mediocre intellectual existence, even though in point of fact I adopt that pose merely as a prophylactic, as if I were a wary libertine moving around in an AIDS-infected milieu—or, to be more precise, as if I had been one, as it's been a long, long time since I was a mediocre intellectual, or any sort of intellectual at all: I am nothing. *I was born a private person*, as J.W.G. once said, and I have remained a private survivor, I say; I am at most still a bit of a literary translator, if I am and have to be anything. As such, despite the threatening circumstances, in the end I radically removed from my path the ignominious existence of a successful Hungarian author, even though, as my wife (for a long time now someone else's wife) told me, I have all the endowments it takes to be one (which slightly horrified me at the time), not that she was saying, my wife said, that I should jettison my *artistic* or any other principles, she was merely saying, my wife said, that I should not be *faint-hearted*, and the more that I was so, that is to say the less I were to do that (jettison my *artistic* or any other principles), the harder I would have to strive to realize those principles, which is to say, when all is said and done, myself, and hence to succeed, my wife said, since everyone strives for that, even the world's greatest authors. "Don't delude yourself," my wife said, "if you don't want success, then why bother writing at all?" she asked, and that is undoubtedly a thorny question, but the time is not yet ripe for me to digress on that; and the sad thing is that she probably saw straight into my heart, she was probably absolutely right, I probably do (did) have all the endowments it takes for the ignominious existence of a successful Hungarian author, the transparent refinements of which I saw through all too clearly, and the flair needed to carry it off is (was) certainly there within me, or if not, then I could acquire (could have acquired) it if I were to transmute my total insecurity and my total fear of existence into simple, blind, unrestrained, agitated and not so much captivating as at most somewhat eye-catching self-adulation, transform them into a moralizing paranoia and unremitting prosecutor of criminal proceedings against others; what is more, and even more dangerous, I had within me in even greater measure the flair needed for the equally ignominious existence of a Hungarian author who is not successful, indeed unsuccessful—and here again I find myself clashing with my wife, who again was the one who got it right, because once one steps onto the path of success then one will be either successful or unsuccessful, *there is no third way*, though certainly both are equally ignominious, albeit in different ways, which is why, for a while, I escaped altogether, as a surrogate for alcoholism, into the objective stupors of literary translation . . . And thus it was that when my wife's words came to mind, my wife too came to mind, though it had been a long time since she had been wont to come to mind, as a matter of fact she does not even come to mind on those rare occasions when we meet, intentionally or unintentionally—more likely intentionally, and almost invariably on the instigation of my (ex-) wife, who, I suppose, must feel some sort of detached, totally groundless sense of guilt mixed with nostalgia towards me, as I see it, to the extent that I notice, and on such occasions I suppose she must be feeling, if anything, a nostalgia for her own youth and the few short years she squandered on me, whereas her totally groundless sense of guilt may be elicited by her awareness of being right—indisputable but then never in dispute and for that very reason gained without the requisite resistance, so to speak, or in other words, the fact that I had never accused her of anything; but then—God help us!—what would I, or could I, have accused her of anyway, except, perhaps, of wanting to live? So, while her words came to mind, she too came to mind, my whole ill-starred and short-lived marriage came to mind, it came to mind and I saw it before me as if it were laid out on a dissection table. And if I look it over, tenderly, lovingly, but in any case with a cool expert eye, the way that, when all is said and done, I prefer to look at everything, even the long stone-cold cadaver of my marriage, then I must guard against forging any cheap, grubby little victories for myself out of my wife's above-quoted words, which as a spouse I undoubtedly listened to, how shall I put it, with irritation; however, on this all-illuminating night, when I see my marriage at such a remove from myself, and I comprehend so little that my incomprehension finally turns out to be quite simple and perfectly comprehensible, on this all-illuminating night, then, I am obliged to recognize that it was my wife's *instinct for life* that drove her to utter those words, and her instinct for life needed my success to make her forget the mighty slice of bad luck that her birth had dealt her, the hated, incomprehensible, unacceptable, absurd bad luck that I myself noticed about her, instantly and, so to say, involuntarily—true, not as bad luck, on the contrary, virtually as a sort of halo, no, that's an exaggeration, let's just say as the nacreous, delicate scallop shell of an incarnation—the moment we first met in an apartment somewhere at a so-called gathering, when all at once she separated from the chattering group as from some hideous, formless, yet nevertheless, because it breathed like living flesh, perhaps kindred matrix, which rippled, expanded and spasmodically contracted as if in the throes of labor; so when she, as it were, broke away from there and traversed a greenish-blue carpet as if she were making her way on the sea, leaving behind her the dolphin's slit open body, and stepped triumphantly yet timidly ever closer towards me, I, let me tell you, instantly and so to say involuntarily thought: "What a lovely Jewish girl!" And even nowadays it still happens that when—albeit very rarely, and almost invariably on the instigation of my (ex-) wife—we meet somewhere, and I look at the way her head is bent forwards, the thick, lustrous hair cascading by her cheeks, as she fills out, on the small coffee-bar table, one after another, the prescriptions for tranquilizers, hypnotics, soporifics and stupefacients that allow me to stick it out for as long as I have to stick it out, and if I have to stick it out, then at least to numb me when seeing, hearing and feeling what I have to see, hear and feel; for—and I didn't mention this before, but then why would I have mentioned it, as I know anyway, so why do I pretend that these jottings concern anyone else but me, though they do, of course—I write because I have to write, and if one writes, one *engages in a dialogue*, I read somewhere; as long as a god existed, probably one *engaged in a dialogue* with God, but now that He no longer exists most likely one can only *engage in a dialogue* with other people or, in the better case, with oneself, or in other words talks or mumbles, as you like, to oneself—anyway, I didn't mention before that my wife (long since someone else's wife) is a physician—well, not in a big way, because I could never have stuck that out, not even for a short time: she is only a dermatologist, though she herself takes it seriously, like everything else; yes, and while she is filling out my prescriptions (because I am devious and deceitful enough to capitalize on and profit from our occasional, entirely innocent rendezvous), even now I still sometimes think: "What a lovely Jewish girl!" Oh, but then how do I think of it now, languidly, feeling sorry, sorry for myself, for her, for everyone and everything, lamentably, no, not that way, not the same way at all as when I then thought "What a lovely Jewish girl!"; yes, this way, the way I thought of it then, naturally and shamelessly, my male member throbbing, like one of those male swine would think of it, a macho, a Jew-baiter, like all those other shameless bastards who think things like: What a lovely Jewish girl, What a lovely gypsy girl, What a classy black woman, French women, Women with glasses, old man, Great tits, Great ass, Small tits, but what a great ass, and so on and so forth. What is more, and had I been unaware of it before, then I was put wise to it that *by no means* just male swine, not at all, but female swine too think exactly, but exactly, *the same way*, or exactly the same way except in reverse, which, when all is said and done, comes to exactly the same thing, as I learned a good while ago in a coffee bar, lit like an aquarium, where I happened to be waiting for my (ex-) wife, and two women, two attractive young women, were talking at a nearby table, and the world all at once went into a spin for a split second, hurling and slamming me back in an almost literal sense with a sudden, gut-wrenching, free-falling sensation to my distant childhood and a long-standing obsession of mine, the origin of which was a sight that was—how can I put it?—startling, but startling because it elicited a lifelong startlement, a sight with which I later—who knows why? but then who could know the transparent secrets of the soul? and if one did know, who would not try to rid himself of them, for they are not just repugnant but also tedious—a sight with which I was later to identify myself so closely on occasions that, even if not in actual reality, to use that meaningless trope, all the same I almost felt I was being transformed into that sight, that *I* was the sight, just the way I saw it in that dusty Lowland village where I had been sent for my summer holiday. Yes, it was there that I lived for the first time among Jews, I mean among genuine Jews, not the kind of Jews *we* were, urban Jews, Budapest Jews, which is to say no kind of Jews, though not Christians either of course, but the kind of non-Jewish Jews who still fast on the Day of Atonement, at the very least up to noon; no, the "aunt" and "uncle" (I no longer remember exactly how we were related, but then why would I remember, they long ago dug their graves in the sky, into which they were sent up in smoke) were genuine Jews, with prayers in the morning, prayers in the evening, prayers before meals, prayers over the wine, but for all that decent people, albeit unbearably dull of course, for a young boy from Pest, their heavy grease-laden fare, goose, bean cholent, and larded, spicy apple *flódni* flatcakes: I think the war had already broken out, but here *at home*, everything was still nice and peaceful, they were still only conducting blackout drills and Hungary was an island of peace in a Europe in flames, what had happened and went on happening uninterruptedly in, let's say, Germany or Poland, or in, let's say, the "Bohemian Protectorate" or France or Croatia or Slovakia, in short everywhere all around, *couldn't happen here*, no, not here, no way; yes, and one morning I carelessly opened the door to enter the bedroom then promptly turned straight back, not noisily, just screaming inside, because I had seen something repellent that struck me as an obscenity and that, purely on account of my age, I was simply unprepared for: *a bald-headed woman was seated in front of the mirror in a red negligee.* And time had to pass before my horrified and confused mind could reconcile that woman with the aunt whom at other times, and indeed right after what had happened, I had been accustomed to seeing with a head of oddly wispy and stiff but otherwise normal russet-tinted brown hair; I did not dare utter a squeak after that, let alone inquire about it, I hoped with all my might that maybe she had not noticed that I had seen her; I lived in a dark, heavy atmosphere of repulsion and secrets, the aunt stripped bare, with her shiny pate like that of a mannequin in a window display, summoned up in me an image now of a corpse, now of a great harlot into whom she transformed herself for the night in the bedroom; and only much later, by which time I was back home, of course, did I dare to raise the question of whether I had rightly seen what I did see, because by then I myself was beginning to have doubts about it and I was not reassured at all by my father's laughing face because, I don't know why, but I sensed his laughter was flippant, flippant and destructive, even if only self-destructive, though at the time—(I was only a child, after all) words like that were still foreign to my vocabulary, I simply found his laughter inane because he did not grasp my terror, my repulsion, the first big, spectacular metamorphosis in my life, whereby in place of the familiar aunt *a bald-headed woman was seated in front of the mirror in a red negligee*, no, he did not grasp the horror of it at all but instead crowned it with further horrors, admittedly in a very good-humored way, by explaining it all, and I understood nothing of the whole explanation except the unclean horror of the facts, or to be more precise, the naked, mysterious and inscrutable factuality of the facts, when he explained that the relatives were *Poylish*, and that *Poylish* women, for religious reasons, shave their hair off and wear a wig, or *shaytl*; then later on, when it started to assume increasing importance that I too was Jewish, since, as gradually became common knowledge, this generally carried a death sentence, probably just so that I should see this incomprehensible and peculiar fact—(namely, that I was Jewish) in all its singular oddity, or at least in a more familiar light, I suddenly realized that I now understood who I was: *a bald-headed woman seated in front of the mirror in a red negligee.* The matter was plain enough, albeit not pleasant and, above all, none too readily comprehensible, but in the final analysis, indisputably, it admirably defined my not pleasant and, above all, none too readily comprehensible situation, to say nothing of my kinship. In the end, as things turned out, I simply no longer needed it because I came to terms with the notion, that is, the notion of my Jewishness, just as I have come to terms, slowly and one by one, with a succession of other not pleasant and, above all, none too readily comprehensible notions, in a sort of crepuscular truce, of course, knowing full well that even these not pleasant and, above all, none too readily comprehensible notions will themselves eventually cease when I cease to be, until which time those notions are admirably useful things, including, in the front rank, the notion of my Jewishness—of course, solely as a not pleasant and, above all, none too readily comprehensible matter of fact, moreover one which now and again is also somewhat life-imperiling, but then, at least for me (and I hope, indeed am confident, that *by no means* everybody will agree with me on this, while I suppose some will be offended at, indeed I sincerely hope will hate, me for this, especially Jewish and non-Jewish philo- and anti-Semites)—as I say, for me its utility resides precisely in this, this is the only way in which I can use it, no other way: as a not pleasant and, above all, none too readily comprehensible and, moreover, occasionally life-imperiling matter of fact that perhaps, purely for its perilousness, *one must try to love*, as we know, though speaking for myself I see no reason for it, perhaps because I long ago stopped trying to live as it were in harmony with other people, with Nature, or even with myself, and what is more, I would see that as nothing short of a form of moral poverty, the same sort of disgusting perversity as in an oedipal relationship or incest between two hideous siblings. Yes, so there I was sitting and waiting for my (ex-) wife in this coffee bar lit like an aquarium, hoping for a pile of new prescriptions and not even thinking about my not pleasant and, above all, none too readily comprehensible and, moreover, periodically life-imperiling existence, while two women at the nearby table chatted and I, virtually as a reflex, started to eavesdrop since they were attractive women, the one more of a blonde, the other more a brunette, and no matter how much and how often they dismayed me (to say no more than that), surreptitiously, if I pay attention, quietly and closely, to the circulation of my blood and my alarming dreams, as a matter of fact I am still, and even so, surreptitiously fond of attractive women, with an unshakable, incorrigible, I might say natural attraction which, for all it purports to be so banally understandable is nevertheless essentially mysterious, since it has almost nothing to do with me, and to that extent is even outrageous and in any event not so readily dismissed as, let's say, my liking for plane trees, which I like simply for their sprawling, blotchy trunks, their splendid and fantastic branches, and their large, veined leaves, dangling as they do, at the right time of the year, like so many listless hands. And I had barely had a chance to join in, if only as a passive party, their conversation, the confidential, one might say stiflingly whispered tone of which instantly intimated a significant topic, when I heard the following words: ". . . I don't know, but I could never do it with a foreigner . . . A black, a gypsy, an Arab . . ." At this point her voice broke off, but I sensed that she was merely hesitating, my sense of rhythm tipped me off that she was not yet finished, no way, there was something still to come, and I was almost beginning to fidget on my chair because, naturally, I knew very well what was still to come, and I was thinking that if she had to rack her brains over it this long, then I would prompt her myself, when finally she added with great bitterness: ". . . a Jew," and all at once, yet quite unexpectedly, even though I had been counting on the word, waiting for it, watching out for it, almost insisting on it, well anyway, the world all at once went into a spin for a split second, with a sudden, gut-wrenching free-falling sensation, and I thought that if that woman were to look at me now, then I would mutate: *I will be a bald-headed woman in a red negligee in front of the mirror*, there is no escaping that curse, I thought, none, and I can see only one way out, I thought, and that is, I thought, to get up straightaway from the table and either slap the woman, I thought, or screw her. Needless to say, I did neither, just as I don't do so many other things that I have thought, often with reason, that I ought to do, and this was not even one of those categorical imperatives over whose violation I could more justifiably shake my head; my temper had hardly flared up, so to speak, than it was snuffed out, beside which, like stray shadows, several nasty but familiar thoughts were in the offing: Why should I bother to convince either the woman or myself, since I have long been convinced about everything, I do what I have to do, and although I don't know why I have to, I do it anyway in the hope, indeed the knowledge, that there will come a time when there will be no need to have to, and I shall be free to stretch out on my comfortable bed, after they have first made me work hard for it, of course, after they have whistled out the signal for me to dig a grave for myself, and at present, even though so much time has already passed—God help us!—I am still just at the digging stage. Then my wife arrived, and I, my feelings eased, instantly and, so to say, involuntarily thought, "What a lovely Jewish girl!" the way she traversed a greenish-blue carpet as if she were making her way on the sea, and she stepped, triumphantly yet still timidly ever closer towards me for she wanted to speak with me, because she knew that I am who I am, B., writer and literary translator, "a piece" of whose she had read which she *absolutely* had to discuss with me, my (then as yet future but now ex-) wife said, and she was still very young, fifteen years younger than me, though I was not yet really all that old either, but then already quite old enough, as ever. Yes, that is how I see her now, in this night of mine, in my big, all-illuminating, lightning-bright night and also in the dark night that descended upon me later, much later, yes: *Sometimes I wonder why I spend a lonely night dreaming of a song . . . and I am once again with you,* I whistle, amazed that I should be whistling, and "Stardust" at that, which is what we always whistled, even though I am now in the habit of whistling only Gustav Mahler, nothing but Gustav Mahler, his Ninth Symphony. But I suppose this is quite beside the point, unless anyone should happen to be familiar with Mahler's Ninth Symphony, in which case they would be able to surmise from its mood, rightfully and with complete justice, my frame of mind, if they happened to be curious about it and were not willing to make do with the direct disclosures emanating from me, from which the necessary conclusions can likewise be drawn. *When our love was new and each kiss an inspiration . . .*

"No!" something bellows, howls, within me, I don't wish to remember, to dunk let's say ladyfingers instead of petites madeleines (unknown, even as unprocurable articles, in this benighted part of the world) into my cup of Garzon tea mixture, though of course I do wish to remember, willingly or not, I can do nothing else: if I write, I remember, I have to remember, though I don't know why I have to remember, obviously for the sake of knowing, remembering is knowing, we live in order to remember what we know, because we cannot forget what we know, don't worry, children, not out of some kind of "moral duty," no, come off it, it's simply *not at our discretion*, we are not *able*, to forget, that is the way we are created, we live in order to know and to remember, and perhaps, indeed probably, indeed with almost total certainty, the reason why we know and remember is in order that somebody should feel shame on our account if he has gone so far as to create us, yes, we remember for the one who either is or isn't, it doesn't matter, because either he is or he isn't: in the end it comes down to the same thing, the essential point is that we should remember, know and remember, that somebody—anybody—should feel shame on our account and (possibly) for us. Because as far as I am concerned, if I were to set off from my privileged, my ceremonial, I nearly said my sanctified memories, but then, I don't mind, if we are going to use grand words, then so be it: from my memories, sanctified and, indeed, consecrated at the black mass of humanity, then gas would start to leak, guttural voices would croak *Der springt noch auf*, the final *Sh'ma Yisroel* from *A Survivor from Warsaw* would be whimpered, and the tumult of world collapse would raise its din . . . And after that a gentle drizzle of surprise, daily renewed that, would you believe it, I leapt up and so to say concealed again after all, *ich sprang doch auf*, indeed I'm still here, though I don't why, unless it was pure chance, the way I was born, I'm just as much an accomplice to my sticking around as I was to my coming into this world—all right, I concede, a grain more shame attaches to hanging around, especially if one has done one's utmost to hang around, but that's all, nothing more: I wasn't willing to be taken in like other suckers by the general passion and breast-beating claptrap about sticking around, God help us! and *in any case you're always partly to blame*, that's all there is to it, I have stuck around and therefore I am, I thought; no, I didn't even think, I just *was*, simple as that, like a Survivor from Warsaw, like a hanger-on from Budapest who sets no store on his hanging on, who feels no need to *justify* his sticking around, to attach notions of *purpose* to his having hung on, yes, to turn his having hung on into a triumph, however quiet, however discreet and intimate, yet essentially still the only *genuine*, the only *possible* triumph, as the prolonged and propagated perpetuation of this hung-on-to existence, namely my own self, in descendants—in a descendant: you—would be (would have been); no, I didn't think about that, I didn't think that I needed to think about that until this night overtook me, that all-illuminating yet pitch-black night, and the question arose before me (or, to be more precise, behind me, behind my long spent life, since, thank God, it's too late and will now always be too late), the question, yes—as to whether you would be a brown-eyed little girl, with the pale specks of your freckles scattered around your tiny nose? Or else a headstrong boy, your eyes bright and hard as greyish-blue pebbles?—yes, contemplating my life as the potentiality of your being, contemplating it at all, strictly, sadly, without anger or hope, as one contemplates an object. As I said, I didn't think of anything, even though, as I said, I ought to have. Because surreptitiously some kind of mole work was going on here, a grubbing and a machinating that I ought to have known about and, of course, did know about, I just took it to be something other than it really was, though what exactly, I don't know—perhaps some kind of reassuring movement, I suspect, much as a blind old man might suppose the ringing, scraping noise of diggers is the earth-mastering work of sewer laying whereas what they are digging there is a grave, and what is more, a grave specifically for him. In short, I suddenly caught myself writing because I had to write, even though I did not know why I had to, the fact is I noticed that I was working incessantly, one might say with an insane diligence, always working, driven not solely by the need to make ends meet, because even if I did not work *I would still exist*, and if I were existing then I don't know what that would drive me to do, and it is better that I don't know, even if my bones, my guts, have an inkling, to be sure, for the reason why I work incessantly is that while I am working I am, and if I did not work, who knows if I would be, therefore I have to take it seriously because the most deadly serious associations subsist between my continued subsistence and my work, that much is blatantly obvious and not in the least normal, even if there happen to be others, even a fair number of them, who likewise write because they have to write, though not everyone who writes has to write, but in my case there was no getting away from the fact that I had to, I don't know why, but it seems this was the only solution open to me, even if it solves nothing, on the other hand at least it does not leave me in a position of—how shall I put it?—unsolvedness that would compel me to regard it as unsolved even in its unsolvedness and consequently torment me not only by virtue of unsolvedness but also by the shortcomings of this unsolvedness and dissatisfaction over that. In hindsight, I may perhaps have considered writing was an escape (and not entirely groundlessly: at worst I supposed I was escaping in another direction, towards a goal other than the one towards which I was actually escaping and even now increasingly escape), an escape, indeed a salvation, a salvation and absolutely indispensable *demonstration* of myself and, through myself, of my material and moreover, to use grand words, mental world to the one—anyone—who will feel shame on one's account and (possibly) for one; and that night had to ensue for me to see at last in the darkness, to see among other things the nature of my work, which in its essence was nothing more than digging, the continued digging of the grave that others had begun to dig for me in the air and then, simply because they did not have time to finish, hastily and without so much as a hint of diabolical mockery (far from it: just like that, casually, without so much as a look around), they thrust the tool in my hand and left me standing there to finish, as best I could, the work that they had begun. And so all my flashes of recognition were merely recognitions leading towards this recognition, and whatever I did, it all became just a recognition within me that led to this recognition—my marriage, just as much as the fact that I said

"No!" instantly and at once, without hesitation and virtually instinctively, yes, still instinctively, for the time being merely instinctively, albeit with instincts that ran counter to my natural instincts, which, however gradually, would (did) become my natural instincts and indeed my very nature; so this "no" was not a decision in which I might (might have), let's say, decided freely between a "yes" and a "no"; no, this "no," the decision, was a recognition, but not a decision that I reached or could have reached, rather a decision *about myself*, or not even a decision but a recognition of my verdict, a decision that could be regarded as such only insofar as I did not decide against the decision, which would undoubtedly have been the wrong decision, for how could a person make a decision against his fate, if I may use this pretentious expression, by which (fate, that is to say) one usually takes to mean what one least understands, which is to say oneself, this treacherous, this unknown, this perpetually countervailing factor that in this form, strange and estranged, as it were bowing in disgust before its power, one nevertheless finds simplest to call one's fate. And if I wish to see my life as more than just a series of arbitrary accidents succeeding the arbitrary accident of my birth, which would be—how shall I put it?—a rather unworthy view of life after all, but rather as a series of recognitions in which my pride, at least my pride, can find gratification, then the question that assumed an outline in Dr. Obláth's presence, I might even say with Dr. Obláth's assistance—*my existence viewed as the potentiality of your being*—now, in the light of that series of recognitions and in the shadow of the onward march of time, was altered, once and for all, in the following manner: *your non-existence viewed as the necessary and radical liquidation of my own existence.* Because this is the only way in which everything that happened, everything that I did and that was done to me, has any meaning, only this way does my meaningless life have any meaning, including my continuing what I started, to live and write, it doesn't matter which, both together, for my ballpoint pen is my spade, and if I look ahead, it is solely to look backwards, if I stare at a sheet of paper, I see solely into the past: *and she traversed a greenish-blue carpet as if making her way on the sea* since she wished to speak with me because she knew that I am who I am, B., writer and literary translator, a "piece" of whose she had read that she *absolutely* had to talk to me about, she said, and talk about it we did until we talked ourselves into bed—God help us!—and we talked afterwards, and meanwhile too, non-stop. Yes, and I recall she started by asking if I was serious about what I had said in the heat of the discussion that had taken place beforehand; but I don't know what I said, I said, as I really did not know, I had said so many things, and I had been just on the point of departing unnoticed ("à l'anglaise," as they say) because I had been irritated and bored by the foregoing discussion, during which I had said what was said, driven by my habitual and loathsome compulsion to speak, a compulsion that assails me chiefly at times when I would prefer to stay silent, on which occasions the compulsion is nothing other than a vocal silence, a verbalized silence, if I may be allowed to overstate the modest paradox: so remind me, I asked, and she, in a choking, husky voice, sketched out a few purchase points, almost severely, aggressively and altogether with a sense of dark, tense excitement—a sexual charge transposed or sublimated into the intellectual realm, or purely and simply disguised by the intellectual realm, I mused lazily and with that unerring sense of certainty with which one is regularly in error, with that resolute blindness whereby one never recognizes continuity in the momentary, consistency in the accidental or a collision in an encounter from which at least one of the parties is bound to emerge as a limping wreck, a sexual charge, I mused naturally and shamelessly, in the way that we all transpose or sublimate or purely and simply disguise our own sexual charge. Yes, and especially now that in my dark, unfathomable night I see rather than hear that social discourse, I see the gloomy faces around me, but only as so many theatrical masks bearing their various roles, those of the weeper and the joker, the wolf and the lamb, the monkey, the bear, the crocodile, and this whole menagerie was murmuring quietly in some huge ultimate swamp where the protagonists, as in one of Aesop's horror fables, were still drawing the final lesson, and someone came up with the melancholy idea that everyone should say *where he had been*, at which the names began to drop with a weary spattering, like rain from a passing cloud which has long ago spent its force: Mauthausen, the Don Bend, Recsk, Siberia, the Transit Centre, Ravensbrück, Fő Street, 60 Andrássy Avenue, the internal resettlement villages, the post-56 jails, Buchenwald, Kistarcsa . . . by now I was dreading it would be my turn, but fortunately I was preempted: "Auschwitz," said somebody in the modest but self-assured tones of a winner, and the whole gathering nodded furiously: "Untrumpable," as the host himself admitted, half enviously, half grudgingly, and yet, when all is said and done, with a wry smile of acknowledgment. Later on the title of a modish book of that period was brought up, a book with a sentence that was modish then, indeed is so to this day and in all likelihood always will be, that the author, after proper but, of course, quite futile clearing of the throat, in a voice still hoarse with emotion, declares "There is no explanation for Auschwitz"—just that, tersely, intensely, swallowing quietly, and I remember how, to my amazement, this gathering of, after all, for the most part hardheaded people accepted, analyzed and debated this simplistic statement, scrutinizing it this way and that, with eyes blinking slyly or hesitantly or uncomprehendingly from behind their masks, as if this declaration to nip all declarations in the bud was actually declaring something, though you do not have to be a Wittgenstein to notice that in point of linguistic logic alone it is flawed and reflects at most certain desires, a false or frankly infantile morality and sundry suppressed complexes but apart from that has no declarative value whatsoever. I believe I actually said so too, after which I just talked and talked, unstoppably, to the verge of logorrhea, taking note from time to time of a woman's gaze that was fixed on me as if seeking to tap a source deep inside me; and, in the thick of my compulsive need to speak, what sprang fleetingly and quite possibly faultily, reflecting at most certain desires and sundry suppressed complexes—as I say, what sprang to mind is that it had been her, the woman who later on became my wife but before that my lover, whom I got to know only after that conversation, when, tired, embarrassed and forgetting all, I had been just on the point of departing unnoticed ("à l'anglaise," as they say) and she traversed a greenish-blue carpet as if she were making her way on the sea. I don't even recall what I said, though obviously I gave vent to my opinion, which obviously cannot have changed much since then, if indeed it has changed at all, which I find very hard to believe, except nowadays I am not much given to venting my opinions, whence perhaps my vague doubts regarding my opinion; but then to what end, and to whom, would I give vent to my opinion, and above all where, since I don't lodge permanently in holiday homes in some mediocre mid-Hungarian hill range in order to cope with the nonpassing of time by giving vent to opinions in the company of Dr. Obláth and high intellects of his ilk—not at all, I reside permanently, or near-permanently, in a one-and-a-half room doodah, there, I nearly said it: apartment, God forgive me—my apartment—my now sun-baked, now wind-buffeted (and sometimes both together) lair on the fourteenth floor of a tower block, looking up from time to time into the brilliant air or at the clouds in which I am digging my grave with my ballpoint pen, diligently, like a forced laborer who is whistled up every day to drive the spade deeper, to play death on the violin with a darker, sweeter tone; here I would be able to vent my opinion, at best, to the thrumming water pipes, the rattling heating pipes and the howling neighbors, here in this tower block in the heart of the Józsefváros district of Budapest, or rather not its heart but its entrails, a block that is so conspicuous, so startling, like an oversized artificial limb, in this ground-hugging neighborhood, but from my window I can at least peek over the (what a surprise!) still extant old fence, and see the pitiful secret of a paltry garden which was a constant source of excitement in my childhood but now excites me not at all, indeed distinctly bores me, as indeed does the thought that, due to certain circumstances (my divorce, my predilection for the worst yet not necessarily the simplest solutions, and then too the fact that the money doesn't exactly roll in), so anyway due to certain circumstances I have ended up back here, in the place where I spent a number of miserable childhood summer and winter vacations, where I gained a number of miserable childhood experiences, so the thought that I am again living here, as long as I still have to live, fourteen floors above my childhood, and therefore inevitably, and now purely for my annoyance, sometimes assails me in the form of totally superfluous memories of my childhood, for surely these memories long ago fulfilled the function that they had to fulfill, their stealthy rat work, eroding everything, gnawing away at everything, they could safely have left me in peace by now. But to get back to . . . what was it? . . . to my opinion—God help us!—I most probably must have said that this statement, which is to say the statement "There is no explanation for Auschwitz," is faulty in purely formal terms, since for something that *is* there is always an explanation, even if, of course, merely an arbitrary, erroneous, so-so kind of explanation; nevertheless, it is a fact that a fact has at least two lives, one a factive life and another, so to say, cerebral life, a cerebral mode of existence, and this is none other than an explanation, the explanations or, better still, set of explanations that overexplain the facts to death, which is to say ultimately annihilate or at least obscure the facts, and this hapless statement that "There is no explanation for Auschwitz" itself is an explanation, being used by its hapless author to explain that it would be better for us to remain silent about Auschwitz, that Auschwitz does not (or did not) exist, because, you see, the only thing for which there is no explanation is something that does not or did not exist. However, I most probably said, Auschwitz did—that is, *does*—exist, and therefore there is also an explanation for it; what there is no explanation for is that there was no Auschwitz, that is to say, it would be impossible to hit upon an explanation for Auschwitz not coming into being, for the state of the world being such as not to be reified in the fact we call "Auschwitz" (if I may be allowed at this juncture to pay my respects to Dr. Obláth); yes, there would be no explanation precisely for an absence of Auschwitz, from which it follows that Auschwitz has been hanging around in the air since long ago, who knows, perhaps for centuries, like dark fruit ripening in the sparkling rays of innumerable disgraces, waiting for the moment when it may at last drop on mankind's head, for in the end what is is, and the fact that it is is necessary because it is: The history of the world presents us with a rational process (quotation from H.), because were I to see the world as a series of arbitrary accidents, then that world would have, well, a rather unworthy view (self-quotation), so let's not forget: To him who looks upon the world rationally the *world* in turn presents a rational aspect: the relation is mutual—again something H. said, not H., Leader and Chancellor, but H., grand-scale visionary, philosopher, court jester and head butler of choice morsels to leaders, chancellors and other titled usurpers, who, I fear, was moreover absolutely right about this, all that is left for us is to examine closely the subsidiary question of *what kind* of rational process it is of that world history presents to us and, furthermore, *whose* rationality looks rationally upon the world in order that the relation may be—as indeed, I'm sorry to say, it is—mutual, I most probably said; the explanation for Auschwitz, I most probably must have said, to my way of thinking the explanation for Auschwitz, I most probably must have said, since that was and indeed still is my opinion, is inherent in individual lives, solely in individual lives; Auschwitz, to my way of thinking, is a rational process of individual lives, viewed in terms of a specific organized condition. If mankind were to start dreaming as a whole, that dream would necessarily be Moosbrugger, the good-natured sex killer, as we can read in Musil's *The Man Without Qualities*, I most probably said. Yes, individual lives, as a whole, and then the whole mechanics of carrying them through, that's all there is to the explanation, nothing more, nothing else, *all things possible do happen; only what happens is possible*, says K., the great, the sad, the wise one, who already knew from individual lives exactly what it would be like when criminal lunatics look upon the world rationally and the world in turn presents a rational aspect to them, that is to say, is obedient to them. And don't tell me, I most probably said, that this explanation is just a tautological way of explaining the facts with facts, because yes, indeed, this explanation, hard as I know it may be for you to accept, that we are governed by commonplace felons—hard even when you already call them commonplace felons and know them as such—nevertheless as soon as a criminal lunatic ends up, not in a madhouse or penal institution, but in a chancellery or other government office you immediately begin to search for what is interesting, original, extraordinary, and (though you don't dare to say so, except in secret, of course) yes, great in him, so you are not obliged to see yourselves as such dwarfs, and histories of the world as so absurd, I most probably said; yes, so that you may continue to look upon the world rationally and the *world* in its turn may present a rational aspect to you. And that is entirely understandable, even entirely commendable, even if your method is neither "scientific" nor "objective," as you would like to believe, it is not; it is sheer lyricism and moralizing insofar as it seeks to restore a rational, or in other words endurable, world order, and those who have been banished from the world subsequently edge their way back into the *world* again through these back and front doors—anyone, that is, who is inclined to do so and who believes that the *world* will henceforth be a place fit for people, but then that is quite another matter, I most probably must have said, the only problem is that this is how legends are born, we can learn from these "objective" lyrical works, these scientific horror stories, say, that the great man had an outstanding tactical sense—right?—as if an outstanding tactical sense were not precisely the means by which every paranoid and manic madman misleads and befuddles those around him and his doctors, and then that social conditions were such-and-such, while international politics were such-and-such, and then some, once philosophy, music and other forms of artistic hocus-pocus had corrupted people's capacity to think, but above all that, when it comes down to it, the great man, let's not mince words, was a *great man*, he had about him something of the disarming, the fascinating, in short: something of the *demonic*, that's it, a demonic streak that was quite simply irresistible, especially if we have no will to resist, seeing that we just happen to be hunting for a demon; a demon is just what we've been needing for a long, long time for our squalid affairs, to gratify our squalid desires, the sort of demon, of course, who can be persuaded to believe that *he* is the demon who will take all our own demoniacality on his shoulders, an Antichrist bearing the Iron Cross, and will not insolently slip through our fingers to string himself up before time, as Stavrogin did. Yes, you see and label them as common criminal lunatics, yet from the moment one lays his hands on the orb and scepter you immediately start to deify him, reviling him even as you deify him, listing the objective circumstances, reciting what, *objectively*, he was right about, but what, *subjectively*, he was not right about, what *objectively* can be understood, and what *subjectively* cannot, what sorts of hanky-panky were going on in the background, what sorts of interests played a part, and never running short of explanations just so that you can salvage your souls and whatever else is salvageable, just so that you can view commonplace robbery, murder and trafficking in souls in which we all, all of us sitting here, somehow play or have played a part, one way or another, in the grand opera-house limelight of world events, I most probably must have said, yes, just so that you may fish partial truths out of the great shipwreck in which *everything whole has been smashed*, yes, just so as not to see before you, behind you, underneath you and at every turn the yawning chasm, the nothingness, the void, or in other words, our true situation, what it is you are serving and the prevailing nature of the prevailing régime, a dominating power which is neither necessary nor unnecessary but simply a matter of decisions, decisions that are made or not made in individual lives, neither satanic nor unfathomably and spellbindingly intricate, nor something that majestically sweeps us up with it, no, it is just vulgar, mean, murderous, stupid, hypocritical, and even at the moments of its greatest achievements at best merely well organized, I most probably must have said; yes, first and foremost, *frivolous*, because ever since the machines of murder have been uncovered here, there and in so many other places, ever since then it has been the end, the end for a good while, of any seriousness that might be taken seriously, at least in respect of the notion of domination, any sort of domination. And just stop once and for all, I most probably said, this "There is no explanation for Auschwitz," that Auschwitz was a product of irrational, incomprehensible forces, because there is always a rational explanation for evil, it may be that Satan himself, just like Iago, is irrational, but his creatures are very much rational beings, their every action may be deduced, in the same way as a mathematical formula may be deduced, from some interest, greed for profit, indolence, lust for power and sex, cowardice, the need to gratify some urge or other or, if nothing else, then, in the final analysis, from some form of madness, paranoia, manic depression, pyromania, sadism, erotomania, masochism, demiurgic or other form of megalomania, necrophilia and what do I know which of the multitude of perversions, perhaps all of them at once, whereas, I most probably must have said, now pay attention, what is truly irrational and genuinely inexplicable is not evil but, on the contrary, good. That is precisely why I have long since had no interest in leaders, chancellors and other titled usurpers, however much you may be able to recount about their inner worlds; no, instead of the lives of dictators, for a long time now I have been interested solely in the lives of saints, because they are what I find interesting and incomprehensible, they are what I am unable to find merely rational explanations for; and even in this respect Auschwitz, however sick a joke this may sound, Auschwitz proved a fruitful enterprise, so however much it may bore you, I will tell you a story, and then you explain it to me, if you can. As I'm sitting in front of a roomful of old hands, I shall be brief, and if I say no more than *Lager*, and winter, and a hospital transport, and cattle wagons, and a single issue of cold food rations, when the journey will last for who knows how many days and the rations are doled out in tenths, and, lying on the wooden contraption that passed for my stretcher, I could not take my dog-eyes off a man, or rather skeleton, who, I have no idea why, was only ever referred to as "Teacher" and who had picked up my ration too, and then the entrainment, and of course, time after time, the roll call doesn't tally, and a yelling and commotion and a kick, then I feel myself being snatched up and dumped in front of the next wagon, and it's a long, long while since I saw either "Teacher" or my ration—that's enough for you to picture the situation precisely. Likewise how I felt: first of all, I had nothing to feed my eternal tormentor, hunger, the irascibly voracious wild beast that had long since become a stranger to me, and now hope, that other wild beast, had begun to rage as well, having hitherto purred faintly, muffled maybe, but insistently, that, all appearances to the contrary, there was still a chance of staying alive. Except that with the ration gone this all at once looked extremely dubious, while on the other hand, and I clarified this cold-bloodedly to myself, my ration would precisely double "Teacher's" chances—so much for my ration, I thought—how shall I put it?—not overjoyed but all the more soberly. Yet what should I see a few minutes later? Calling out and looking frantically all around, "Teacher" was staggering towards me, a single issue of cold rations in his hand, and when he glimpses me on the stretcher he quickly places it on my stomach; I am about to say something, and it seems that astonishment must be written all over my face because he, though already scurrying back—if they don't find him in his place they will simply beat him to death—he says, with clearly recognizable signs of indignation on his little face, already preparing for death, "You didn't imagine for one moment . . . ?" So much for the story, and even if it were true that I do not wish to see my life merely as a series of arbitrary accidents succeeding the arbitrary accident of my birth, because that would indeed be a rather unworthy view of life, I have still less wish to see things as though they had all happened in order that I should stay alive, since that would, perhaps, constitute an even more unworthy view of life, although there's no getting round the fact that "Teacher," for example, did what he did in order that I should stay alive, to look at it purely from my viewpoint, of course, because he himself was plainly guided by something else, plainly it was primarily to preserve his own life that he did what he did, only incidentally to preserve my life too. And the question here, and find me an answer to it if you can, is why he did that. But don't try putting it into words, for you know as well as I do that under certain circumstances, at a certain temperature, metaphorically speaking, words lose their substance, their content, their meaning, they simply deliquesce, so that in this vaporous state deeds alone, naked deeds, show any tendency to solidity, it is deeds alone that we can take in our hands, so to speak, and examine like a mute lump of mineral, like a crystal. And if we take as our starting-point (and clearly there is no other point from which we can start, is there?) that in an extreme situation such as a concentration camp, and giving particular consideration to the total breakdown of body and mind, and the resulting almost pathological atrophy of the faculty of judgment, what generally guides anyone is solely one's own staying alive, and furthermore, if you think about it, that "Teacher" had been offered a twofold chance of staying alive, yet he *rejected* that doubled chance, or to be absolutely precise, an extra chance on offer over and above his own chance, which, in point of fact, represented someone else's chance, this suggests that precisely the—how shall I put it?—very acceptance of that second chance would also have nullified the *sole* chance he still had to live and stay alive; so according to this there *is* something, and I can again only ask that you don't try putting names to it, there *exists* a pure concept, untrammeled by any foreign matter, such as our body, our soul or our wild selves, a notion which lives as a uniform image in all our minds, yes, an idea whose—how shall I put this?—inviolability, safekeeping, or what you will, was for him, "Teacher," the *sole genuine chance* of staying alive, without which his chance of staying alive would have been no chance at all, simply because he did not wish, and what is more, in all likelihood, was *unable*, to live without preserving this concept intact in its pure, untrammeled openness to scrutiny. Yes, and in my opinion *this* is what there is no explanation for, since it is not rational as compared with the tangible rationality of an issue of food rations, which in the extreme situation called a concentration camp might serve to avoid the ultimate end, if it could serve that purpose, if that service did not run up against the resistance of an immaterial concept which sweeps even vital interests to the side, and this, in my opinion, is a most important testimony for fates in that great metabolism of what, in point of fact, constitutes life—much, so much more important than the banalities and rational acts of terror that any leader, chancellor or other titular usurper ever offered or could offer, I most probably said . . . But I am becoming bored with my own stories, though I don't repudiate them and I can't stay silent about them either, because it is my business to tell them, though I don't know why it is my business, or to be more precise, why I feel as if it were my business, when of course I have no business in the whole wide world, since all my business here on earth has come to an end and merely one thing still remains for me, we all know what that is, and that will not be up to me, no, truly not; and now that I study my stories from the rear, so to say, from afar, wistfully, like the smoke curling upwards from my cigarette, I see a woman's gaze fixed on me as if seeking to tap a source from within me, and in the luminance of this gaze I suddenly understand, I understand and almost see how my stories are braided into twisting threads, soft hooks woven from colored threads that I cast around the waist, breasts and throat of my (then still future, but now ex-) wife, but before that my lover, lying in my bed, her silky head resting on my shoulder, ensnare her and bind her to myself, spinning and twisting, two agile, motley circus performers who will later take their bows, deathly pale and empty-handed, before that jeering spectator, failure. But—yes—*we must at least have the will to fail*, as Bernhard's scientist says, because failure, failure alone, is left as the sole fulfillable experience, I say, and thus I too have the will, if I must have a will to anything, and I must, because I live and write, and both are willings, life being more a blind willing, writing more a sighted willing and therefore, of course, a different kind of willing from life, maybe it has the will to see what life has the will for, because it can do nothing else, it recites life back to life, recapitulates life, as if it, writing, were itself life, though it is not, quite fundamentally, incommensurably, indeed incomparably not that, hence if one starts to write, and one starts to write about life, failure is guaranteed. And now, in my bottomless night, rent by lights, sounds and the pains throbbing inside me, I seek answers to the final, big questions, knowing full well all the while that to every final, big question there exists just a single final, big answer: the one that solves all things because it stills all questions and all questioners, and for us, ultimately, this is the sole existing solution, the final goal of our willings, even if ordinarily we take no notice of it and don't in any way have the will for it, for then we would have no will at all, though speaking for myself I don't see what purpose might still be served by quibbling; nevertheless, while I am recapitulating my life here—God help us!—this life here, and I ask myself why I bother, apart from having to work, maniacally, with lunatic diligence and without a break, because associations of mortal seriousness are sustained between my continued sustenance and my work, that's perfectly obvious, all the same, recapitulating my life here, I am probably driven by some surreptitious hope of my surreptitious will, namely, that I might one day become acquainted with this hope, and I shall probably keep on writing, maniacally, with lunatic diligence and without a break, until I have made its acquaintance, because what reason would I have for writing after that? And when later on, as the pair of us roamed the dingy and not so dingy streets, my wife (to-be and ex-) asked what name I would give, all the same, to that particular pure concept, untrammeled by any foreign matter, about which I had spoken earlier, at the gathering, in connection with "Teacher," who, incidentally, she declared was "a very moving figure" and she hoped she would encounter him again in one of my pieces, she said, a remark to which I turned a blind eye, so to say, as to a physical blemish which should not be allowed to disturb the magic, at least for the moment while the magic still is magic, and without hesitation I rejoined that that concept was, in my opinion, freedom, and freedom primarily because "Teacher" did not do what he *ought* to have done, that is, what he *ought* to have done according to rational calculations of hunger, the survival instinct and madness, and the blood compact that the dominating power had entered into with hunger, the survival instinct and madness, but instead, repudiating all that, he did something else, something that he *ought not* to have done and that no rationally minded person would expect from anybody. At that my wife (though not yet that at the time) fell silent for a while, then suddenly—and I recollect her face upraised to me in the dancing lights of the night, both soft-grained and glassily opalescent and glistening, like a 1930s close-up, and I recollect her voice too, which trembled with the emotion and agitation of her audacity, or at least that was what I supposed at the time, and maybe it was so, though why would it have been since nothing is quite what we suppose or would like to suppose, the world not being a *notion* but a chimera of ours, full of unimaginable surprises—suddenly declared that I must be very lonely and sad and, for all my experience, very inexperienced to be so lacking in faith in people, yes, to need to be producing theories in order to explain a natural (yes, that's what she said: natural), a *natural* and decent human gesture; and I recollect how much these words upset me, a remark that was so utterly amateurish and so beguiling in its very untenability, I recollect, yes, just as I also recollect the smile that followed, timid at first but turning quizzical, then rapidly confidential, a play of expressions that I have tried to conjure up so many times subsequently, because in a certain sense it always entranced me, to start with pleasurably, later, when I no longer managed to conjure it up, painfully; or in other words, to start with its reality, later on its lack, and still later on just its memory, the way it usually is and, it would seem, has to be, as it is never any different—I recollect all this, my emotions suddenly compacting, becoming almost uncomfortably immanent and confused, and even more the question she asked as to whether she might take my arm. "Certainly," I replied. But at this point it would be fitting for me to relate roughly how I was living at the time so that I may understand and recognize what I need to understand and recognize, and that is in what respect this moment differed from other, similar moments in which, just as in that moment, it was decided that I would soon be going to bed with a woman. And I put it this way, "it was decided," because even though it is true—and what could be more natural, naturally—that I myself always play a goodly part in such decisions, even to the extent of taking on the role of prime mover, or at least an appearance of that, nevertheless this practically never presents itself to me as a decision; on the contrary, it presents itself to me as an adventure which renders impossible even the possibility of there being a decision, like a vortex opening at my feet, when my blood is seething inside me like a waterfall, stilling all other considerations, and at the same time I am perfectly clear, well in advance of the usual outcome of the adventure, so that as far as a decision is concerned, if it were to lie within my power, I would hardly decide to commit myself to adventures of this kind. But maybe it is precisely this which attracts me, this contradiction, this vortex. I don't know, I just don't know. Because this has happened to me more than once, the selfsame thing, the selfsame way, so I have to infer from this constant repetition that some sort of pattern is stealthily actuating and guiding me: a woman with a timid smile and scurrying movements, in the archaic guise of a loose-tressed, barefoot serving wench as it were, quietly and modestly asks permission to enter—how shall I put it in order to avoid having to utter the banality that I shall nevertheless utter, because what else could I say, if the cheap trick has proved itself since time immemorial, and splendidly at that?—asks permission to enter my *ultimum moriens*, my ultimate failure, in other words my heart, whereupon she takes a look around with a charming and inquisitive smile, delicately touches everything, dusts down one thing and another, airs the musty crannies, throws out this and that, stows her own stuff in their place, and nicely, tidily, and irresistibly settles in until I finally become aware that she has completely squeezed me out of there, so that boxed in like an outcast stranger I find I am steering clear of my own heart, which now only presents itself to me distantly, with closed doors, like the snug homes of others before the homeless; and very often I have only managed to move back in by arriving hand in hand with another woman and letting her lodge there instead. I carefully thought it all through in this much detail, or this plastically I might say, as only befits my profession as writer and translator, after one of my longer-standing, almost painfully and interminably long-standing relationships had come to an end, a relationship that at the time, or so I believed, was taking a fairly heavy toll on me and, seeing it was thereby threatening the *freedom* that was absolutely necessary (not just necessary: indispensable) for my work, I was induced to prudence yet at the same time to further reflection as to what would follow. That was chiefly because I couldn't help noticing that regaining my long-yearned freedom by no means conferred the stimulus to work that I expected from this turn of events; indeed, I disconcertedly had to admit that I had worked more energetically, I might say more angrily, and thus more productively, while I had merely been struggling for my freedom, indecisively now breaking up, now getting back together again, than I was working now, when I was free again, to be sure, but this freedom only filled me with emptiness and boredom; just as a good deal later, another sort of state, to wit the happiness that I experienced with my wife during our relationship and then at the beginning of our marriage, likewise taught me that this state, to wit that is to say happiness, also has an adverse effect on my work. So first of all I took a hard look at my work, as to what it really is and why it creates demands that are so oppressive, or at any rate tiring and often frankly unattainable, virtually suicidal; and even if I was then still groping far away—God, and how far—from true clear-sightedness, from a recognition of the true nature of my work, which is in essence nothing other than to dig, to keep on digging to the end, the grave that others have started to dig for me in the air; at any rate, I recognized that as long as I am working I am, and if I were not working, who knows, would I be? could I be? so in this way the most deadly serious associations are sustained between my continued sustenance and my work, one precondition of which, it seems, must be, I supposed (because, however sadly this may reflect on me, I was unable to suppose otherwise), unhappiness, though not of course unhappiness of the sort that would immediately deprive me of even the possibility of my working, such as illness, homelessness, poverty, to say nothing of prison and the like, but rather the sort of unhappiness that women alone can confer on me. As a result, and especially since at the time I happened to be reading Schopenhauer's speculation "On the Apparent Deliberateness in the Fate of the Individual," which can be found in one of the volumes of *Parerga and Paralipomena*, a set of which I latched upon as plunder in an antiquarian bookshop during the period of library liquidations following the country's great ethnic upheavals and wave of emigration, moreover so cheaply that even I was able to afford the four bulky black tomes, survivors of censorships, book burnings, pulpings, and all manner of other book-Auschwitzes, as a result I could not entirely rule out the possibility that, to avail myself of that most obsolete expression in wholly obsolete psychoanalysis, I am possibly subject to somewhat of an Oedipus complex, which, after all, taking into account the not exactly orderly circumstances of my younger days, would be little wonder, I supposed now, the only question I asked myself was whether the influence (albeit not the sole determinant, for the mere possibility of this self-analysis was in itself more than encouraging, I supposed) came from the father-son or the mother-son relationship, and the answer I gave myself was that it was most likely the role of the mother's son, the mother's rejected son, that manifests itself now and again in my behavior. I even went so far as to construct a hypothesis around this, as the jottings I made at the time testify. According to this, the father's rejected son inclines more towards a transcendental problematic, whereas the mother's rejected son, and that is what I had to postulate myself as being, tends towards a more sensory, pliable and impressionable material, towards plasticity, and I supposed ready examples of the former were to be found in Kafka, and of the second in Proust or Joseph Roth. And even though this hypothesis probably rests on an extremely shaky footing, and these days I would know better than not only not to write it down but even to bring it up as a topic for a flagging late-night discussion, all the more because it simply no longer interests me (oh, I've moved on a long way since then), and if I still have any recollection of it at all, then it is just as a brief, still aimless and hesitant step on the long, long, who could know how protracted path to true clear-sightedness, or, in other words, conscious self-liquidation; at any rate, it is a fact that the—how shall I put it?—benefit of this complex flowed from me into my work, its harm from my work into me, so I was able to deduce from the apparent deliberateness manifested, if not exactly in my fate, then at least in my behavior at the time, that I furtively produce, verbally create, the situation and role of the mother's rejected son, presumably on account of the accompanying very singular—and, were I not a little ashamed, I would say gratifying—pain, which, from the viewpoint of my work, it seems I absolutely require (naturally, along with *freedom*, which is my prime requirement). Yes, because it appears that in my pain I end up hitting on creative forces, no matter what the price, and no matter that it may just be ordinary compensation finding an outlet in creativity, what is important is that it nonetheless finds an outlet and that through the pain I live in some sort of truth, and if I did not live in it, perhaps the simple truth might—who knows?—leave me cold; as it is, however, the notion of pain is intimately and permanently interwoven within me with the aspect of life, the (I am quite certain) most authentic aspect of life. And in this I then also spotted an explanation for the phenomenon that I was talking about previously, namely, why, when I am in possession of my complete freedom, my stimulus to work is reduced, whereas when I am in the thick of fighting for my freedom and in all sorts of mental turmoil, it is increased, for obviously the way the neurosis induced by my complex (or which induces my complex) affects me is that, if it is in its receding phase, then my desire to work also subsides, but if some new trauma arrives to rekindle the neurosis dormant within me, my desire to work is also ignited. That's perfectly clear and simple, so now one might think all one needs is to provide for continual triggers to keep the fires of my work incessantly burning—and I formulate it in this pointed manner precisely in order to underline its absurdity to myself, because as soon as I had completed this self-analysis I also squared accounts with my complex, indeed, I instantly took a natural aversion to it, or to be more accurate, not only to my complex but also to myself for building up the complex even as I was concealing it from myself and playacting, precisely this idiotic infantile complex, attesting to intellectual immaturity and betraying inadmissible vulnerability, when there is nothing I hate more than infantilism. I was thus cured at least of that particular complex, or to be more precise, I pronounced myself cured, not so much in the interests of regaining my health of course but more my self-esteem, so that when, not long after that, I entered into a relationship with another woman, I laid down the possibly harsh-sounding but nevertheless highly practical condition that the word "love" and its synonyms should never be uttered between us, or in other words, that our love could last only as long as we were not in love with one another, whether mutually or unilaterally was neither here nor there, because the moment that this misfortune should happen to overtake either or, perchance, both of us, we would have to terminate our relationship instantly; and my partner, let me put it that way, who also happened to be recovering from a fairly severe amatory mishap, accepted this condition without demur (at least so it seemed) though the untroubledness of our relationship, I don't doubt it, evidently soon troubled her and would have eroded our relationship had I not in the meantime made the acquaintance of my ex- (or at that time still future) wife, which in the end (at least for me) represented the radical solution. Around this time, moreover, I was still living in a sublet room, which undeniably seemed absurd, so to say, under the circumstances of a consolidation that by then was heading into its second decade, at a time when—albeit usually at the cost of myocardial infarcts, diabetes, chronic gastric ulcers, psychosomatic breakdowns, moral and financial ruin or, in the better cases, merely the total disintegration of family life—nearly all my friends and acquaintances or whatever I might call them had acquired their own apartments, as for me, I didn't think about it, or to the extent that I did think about it I thought that I could not entertain the thought of it, simply because it would have required me to live in a different way, under the badge of money and, above all, of moneymaking, and that would have entailed so many concessions, misconceptions, compromises and, all in all, so much *inconvenience*, even if I were to have lulled myself into thinking that it was all just *temporary*, purely a means to an end, because how can we live even temporarily in any way other than the way we must permanently and generally live without its bitter consequences rebounding on our normal life, that is to say, more or less the life that, after all, we have stipulated for ourselves, in which we are, after all, the masters and legislators, and I was therefore simply unable, and did not even wish, to take upon myself all these absurdities, the absurd inconveniences of acquiring an apartment in Hungary, which first and foremost would have put *my freedom*, my independence of mind and as a matter of fact my independence from external circumstances under threat, under total threat at that, so that I had to set myself against that danger totally, or in other words, with my whole life. And actually I must admit that my wife was right, for after reconnoitering my circumstances at the time with searching tenacity and irresistible probing, accompanied by those plays of expression that were already then slowly becoming familiar and which, so I thought at the time, acted upon me like an ever-surprising and miraculous sunrise, she declared that meant I was imprisoning myself for the sake of my freedom.

Yes, undoubtedly there was some truth in that. To be more accurate, that was precisely the truth. That, given a choice between the prison of acquiring an apartment in Hungary and the prison of not owning an apartment in Hungary, the latter suited me better, since there (in the prison of not owning an apartment in Hungary) I was better able to do as I pleased, better able to live for myself, sheltered, concealed and uncorrupted, until this prison—or, if one insists on making comparisons, I could perhaps better call it a preserving jar—suddenly, and undoubtedly through my wife's magic touch, sprang open, and my subtenant life all at once proved to be unsheltered, unconcealed, corruptible and consequently untenable, just like my subsequent and eventually my present life too, and just as, I suppose, every life proves to be untenable once it is contemplated in the light of our flashes of recognition, for it is precisely the untenability of our lives which leads to our flashes of recognition, in the light of which we come to recognize that our life is untenable—and it really is that, untenable, because it is taken away from us. Yes, I lived my subtenant life as if I were not quite living, diminished, temporarily, absentmindedly (taking only my work seriously), with that feeling, unclarified but sure, and therefore not standing in need of clarification, feeling, that it was, as it were, merely a waiting period of uncertain duration elapsing between my only two pieces of true business, that of my coming into being and that of my passing away, which I must somehow while away (preferably with work); yet this waiting period is my only time, the only time I can account for, though I don't know why and to whom I should account for it, perhaps to myself, above all, so that I may recognize what I still have to recognize and do what I still can do, but then to everybody, or to nobody, or to anybody who will be ashamed on our behalf and possibly for us, since I am unable to account for my time either prior to my coming into being or after my passing away, if these states of mine have anything at all to do with *the only time I have*—something (that is, that they could have anything to do with it) I find hard to believe. And now that, in the clarity of my night as it descends upon me, I contemplate my subtenant life at length and fretfully, with a cool expertise maybe, yet not free from certain preconceptions either, I suddenly believe I recognize its archetype, and more specifically believe I recognize it in my concentration camp life not so many years, though also an eternity ago; to be precise, in that phase of my camp life when my camp life was no longer real camp life, insofar as liberating soldiers had taken the place of the incarcerating soldiers, yet it was camp life all the same because I was still living in a camp. It happened precisely the day after this change in state (that is, that liberating soldiers had replaced the incarcerating soldiers) that I staggered out of the hospital barrack *Saal*, or room, in which I was then quartered, since I was, to put it mildly, ill, which in itself of course hardly constituted grounds for my being accommodated in the hospital barrack but, owing to a coincidence of certain circumstances which, in the final analysis, took the form of a piece of good luck only slightly more astounding than the accustomed bad luck, I nevertheless happened to be being accommodated in the hospital barrack, and the next morning I staggered out of the *Saal*, or room, to the so-called ablutions, and as I opened the door to the so-called ablutions and was just about to move towards the wash trough, or perhaps before that to the urinal, when my feet simply (and I am unable to come up with anything more apt than this tired cliché, because that was almost literally what happened) they simply became rooted to the spot, for *a German soldier was standing at the washbasin and as I entered he slowly turned his head toward me*; and before fright could cause me to collapse, faint, wet myself or who knows what else, through the greyish-black fog of my terror I noticed a gesture, a hand gesture by the German soldier, beckoning me towards the washbasin, a rag that the German soldier was holding in the hand that was making the gesture, and a smile, the German soldier's smile; in other words, I slowly grasped that *the German soldier was just scrubbing the washbasin*, while his smile was merely expressing his readiness to be of service to me, that *he was scrubbing the washbasin for me*, or in other words the world order had changed, which is to say that it had not changed at all, which is to say that the world order had changed merely this much, and yet even just that much was not an entirely negligible change in that whereas yesterday it had been I who was the prisoner, today it was he, and this put an end to my sudden terror only inasmuch as it gradually tamed the immediate feeling into one of persistent and unshakable mistrustfulness, matured it within me, one could say, into a way of looking at the world that my subsequent camp life (because I continued to live like this, as a free camp inmate in the camp, for quite a while) bestowed on my free camp life such a singular flavor and piquancy, the unforgettably sweet and tentative experience of life regained: that I was living and yet living as if *the Germans might return at any moment*, and therefore not fully living after all. Yes, and I have to believe (though it was probably as yet unknowing, allowing for the circumstances: the constraint of not owning an apartment that, in the final analysis, I prolonged this experience, the unforgettably sweet and tentative experience of my free camp life, into my subtenant life, this experience of a life before and after all flashes of recognition, unencumbered by any of life's burdens, least of all the burden of life itself, that I was living, but living as if the Germans might return at any moment; and if I impart to this notion, or way of life, or whatever I should call it, a certain symbolic significance, it immediately seems it is thus less absurd, for there is no getting away from it, in a symbolic sense, the Germans might return at any moment, *der Tod ist ein Meister aus Deutschland, sein Auge ist blau*, Death is a blue-eyed master from Germany, he can come at any moment, track you down anywhere, take aim at you, and he makes no mistake, *er trifft dich genau*. So that was how I lived my subtenant life, in a way that was not quite living and indisputably not quite a life, rather it was just being alive, yes, *surviving*, to be more precise. Obviously, this subsequently left deeper imprints in me. I suppose certain of my obvious peculiarities also have their roots in this. I suppose I ought to talk here about, for example, my relationship to property, the property that sustains everybody, mobilizes everybody, maddens everybody, about this relationship which is actually nonexistent, or at most existent merely as a pure negativity. I don't believe, and cannot even imagine, that this negativity is a congenital negativity, some kind of defect, otherwise how would I explain my rigid attachment to certain of my more trivial personal chattels (books) or, if it comes to that, to my most important chattel: myself, the fact that I have always sturdily, one might say radically, guarded the chattel I regard as most important (myself), on the one hand against any form of effective self-destruction that is not a decision of my own free will, and on the other hand I have always guarded it, and continue to guard it, indeed increasingly so, against the cheap and perverted seductions of any sort of communal idea (which, by the way, I could just as well list among the varieties of effective self-destruction), even if, of course, I am merely guarding it for another form of destruction; no, I have no doubt that this negative relationship of mine to property was shaped purely by the survival of my survival, by this so very singular and in a certain sense not entirely unproductive, though, of course, sadly untenable mode of existence, which demonstrated my subtenant life to be likewise self-explanatory. In the subtenancy into which I moved during the darkest of those years, which, in accordance with the twisted laws of hell, we were obliged to proclaim incessantly, aloud and in chorus, as the most glittering years, and where I was greeted virtually as a savior, since my presence seemed to protect the sole commandeerable, distrainable, expropriable, billetable, partitionable, requisitionable, etc., etc., room in what was, incidentally, a fairly pleasant apartment, tucked away in a secluded Buda side street, and for which, for that very reason, I had to pay only a virtually symbolic rent that was raised only equally symbolically in the course of subsequent years; as I say, in that subtenancy, neither then, when I could not yet even think about property, nor later, when I could (indeed, perhaps should) have thought about property, yet did not think about it at all, as I say, there I was not threatened by the hazards that are the concomitants of property, the desperate and distressing measures demanded by cracks in pipes, ceilings and elsewhere, the speculations that are the concomitants of property, as to whether or not the property is satisfactory, and ought one not to have at one's disposal more, or at least more satisfactory, property, while of course taking the best possible advantage (i.e., profit) from the existing, unsatisfactory property; no, an obsessional notion of changing could not possibly have occurred to me, that chafing impulse which might continually dangle before me the possibility of imaginary choices, incessantly pester me and hoodwink me into thinking that I could swap my being here for being somewhere else, that I could exchange my tower-block apartment—of course, at the price of the necessary running around, shelling out, official processing and other unforeseeable complications—for a more satisfactory one, when I don't even know what it is that would satisfy me more, since I am not even satisfactorily acquainted with my desires, and that is before saying anything about the insoluble worries over furniture, as a result of which my tower-block apartment even now, after so much time, is still not satisfactorily furnished, for I simply don't know how I should furnish my apartment, I have no conception of an apartment furnished for myself, not the slightest idea what sort of apartment I would like, what sorts of articles I would like to see it furnished with. In my subtenancy, each and every one of the articles was the property of the householders; they were already waiting for me to settle in among them, and in the course of the long, long years that I spent among them perhaps it did not so much as enter my head even to change the place of a single one of the articles, let alone exchange them for other articles or, perhaps, swell their ranks with newer articles purely because, let's say, I saw an article, wanted it and bought it (aside from books, my books, which I placed at first in a cupboard, then, when that was full, on the table, and then, when there was no more room there either, simply on the floor, until the householders themselves supplementally installed a low supplemental makeshift bookcase); no, as I say, I had no desire at all for, did not buy, indeed probably did not even look at articles, for nothing drives me closer to distraction than a shopwindow piled high with articles, those kinds of shopwindows quite literally dispirit, depress, even demoralize me, so, as I said, I do not look at them at all if possible, which is obviously a sign that I can hardly have any demands of this nature, in this realm (the realm of articles) I make do with the bare necessities, as they say, and probably I am most truly grateful to be placed in a ready-furnished setting where all I have to do is to accept, become acquainted with and grow accustomed to the constellation. I think I was born to be the ideal hotel resident, but because times changed all I could be was a resident of camps and subtenancies, I jotted down at the time in my notebook, from which I am now, decades later, copying into this other notebook, somewhat surprised that I was already then jotting down these kinds of things, which clearly shows that even then I was not living completely blind to my situation, to the untenability of this untenable situation and untenable life. Around that time, I remember, I suffered greatly from a feeling (in reality I might better to call it an ailment) which for my own purposes I termed a "sense of strangeness." The sensation has been well known to me from early childhood on, essentially my constant companion in life, but around that time it haunted me in a manner little short of hazardous, not allowing me to work during the day nor allowing me to sleep at night, leaving me at once tense to breaking-point and enervated to the point of inertia. It's a well-defined nervous ailment, not a figment of the imagination, I at any rate believe that in its essence it has a basis in reality, in the reality of our human condition. Usually it starts with what is often an awesome, but sometimes, especially back then, intolerably acute feeling that my life is hanging by a single thread; it's not a matter of whether I am living or dying, death has nothing to do with it, in fact it has to do with nothing other than life, and life alone, it's just that life suddenly assumes within me an aspect and form, or more accurately a formlessness, of the utmost uncertainty, so I am not at all sure about reality; yes, I am seized by total uncertainty about the extremely suspect experiences that are presented to my senses as is for reality, the *real* existence of myself and my surroundings altogether, an existence that, as I have already said, at the time of such experiences or what I might perhaps better call paroxysms, anyway at the time of these paroxysmal experiences, is connected by just a single thread to life, my own and that of my surroundings, and that thread is my reason alone, nothing else. But then, not only is my mind mistake-prone and, to put it mildly, a far from perfect instrument or sensory organ, or whatever I should call it, on top of that it usually functions sluggishly, haltingly, fuzzily, indeed at times hardly at all. It only follows my actions like someone in bed with the flu does *another's* bustling about around him, registering almost everything only after the event, and though one tries to direct this *stranger's* rummaging and activity with the occasional listless word, if the latter pays no attention, or happens not to hear, with a resigned impotence one gives up bothering anymore. Yes, this is the "sense of strangeness," a state of total estrangement which contains not even a slight hint of the fantastical, the astonishing, or an unbridled imagination but just torments one with the tedium of the routine, the commonplace; yes, an utter homelessness, though it neither knows nor gives cognizance of any home, either abandoned or waiting for me in the way that, for example—and this is a question that I have often posed myself in such states—death would be a home, for example. But then, I have replied to myself on such occasions, I ought to believe in the other world, but the snag is precisely that I cannot believe in this world, least of all when in these states, where I am reduced to addressing such questions to myself and when I hold the existence of another world (to wit, the other world) to be just as much an absurdity as the existence of this world; that is to say, I don't hold it to be at all inconceivable, nor yet conceivable, of course, that another world (to wit, the other world) may exist, only that even if it does exist, then it certainly does not exist for *me* because I am *here*. That is, barely here at that; I am only more or less alive, and that fills me with a sense of some unnameable sin. At such times I often tried (try) to sober up, as it were, but in vain; it seems that it is possible for me to connect with life solely in the form of some sort of logical game, like playing chess or making calculations on a piece of paper and, by inscrutable ways and means, all at once some sort of reality derives from the abstract result—in the way (and this was one of my favorite examples at that time, I even noted it down on a pad, from which I am now writing it down here), so in the way, I wrote, let's say, one holds two wires together, screws them down, inserts the other end into a hole in the wall, presses a button, and the lamp burns; what has happened is an entirely conscious calculation of probabilities, I wrote, the result is the expected one but nonetheless amazing and, in a certain sense, incomprehensible, I wrote. Everything, but everything, is mere deduction, conjecture and probability, no certainty anywhere, no shred of proof anywhere, I wrote. What constitutes my existence? Why am I? What is my essence? For all these questions, I wrote, it's common knowledge that it is hopeless for me to seek not the answer so much as merely reliable signs; and even my body, which sustains me and will eventually kill me, is strange, I wrote. "Maybe if for just one moment in my life, just a single moment, it were given to me to live in step, so to speak, with the detoxifying actions of my kidneys and liver, the peristaltic movements of my stomach and intestines, the inhalatory and exhalatory movements of my lungs, the systole and diastole of my heart, as well as the metabolic exchanges of my brain with the external world, the formation of abstract thoughts in my mind, the pure knowledge that my consciousness has of all these things and of itself, and the involuntary yet merciful presence of my transcendental soul; if, for just a single moment, *I might see, know and possess* myself in this way, when there could be no question of course of either possessor or possession, but *my identity* would simply spring into existence, which can never, ever come into existence; if just one such unrealizable moment were to be realized, maybe that would abolish my "sense of strangeness," teach me to *know*, and only then would I know what it means to be. But since that is an impossibility, it being common knowledge that we don't know, and can never know, what *causes* the *cause* of our presence, we are not acquainted with the purpose of our presence, nor do we know why we must disappear from here once we have appeared, I wrote. I don't know why, I wrote, instead of living a life that may, perhaps, exist somewhere, I am obliged to live merely that fragment which happens to have been given to me: this gender, this body, this consciousness, this geographical arena, this fate, language, history and subtenancy, I wrote. And now that I am noting down what I noted down then, one of my nights then is suddenly revived within me, a dream of mine or, to be more accurate, a waking state of mine, or perhaps a waking dream or a dreaming wakefulness, I don't know which, but anyway I recall it in extraordinary detail, as if it had occurred only yesterday. I was woken, or plunged into a dream (I don't know which, and it doesn't matter at all), by a quite unusually acute "sense of strangeness" such as I had never felt before. That too was a brilliant night, like my present night, glistening velvety-black and pervaded by a motionless, mute, but imperturbable consciousness, and I suddenly realized it was virtually a complete impossibility that this incisive, passive consciousness should all of a sudden simply cease to be and disappear from the world. Yes, and it was as though this consciousness were in no way *my* consciousness, more a consciousness *of myself*, and thus while I may know about it, I cannot have it at my disposal, as if, like I say, it were an ever- and omnipresent consciousness not belonging exclusively to me, from which I simply cannot free myself and which, quite fruitlessly and to no purpose, torments me personally to death. On the other hand, I sensed with absolute clarity that this passive consciousness was nonetheless actually not an unhappy consciousness, and that even if I, though only as a subject of that consciousness, were to be unhappy at this moment, that was more a consciousness of my own impotence in relation to that consciousness, in relation to that pitiless, eternal, tormenting, but for all that, as I said, by no means unhappy consciousness; thus, on fully awakening, or plunging fully into my dream (as I said, it really doesn't matter which), it was subsequently impossible for me not to draw inferences as to the mystery, or rather impossible not to reflect at least that this consciousness is a *part* of something that encompasses me too within itself, that it is not of my body yet is not completely of my mind either, even though it is mediated by my mind, that it is therefore not exclusively mine, and in truth this consciousness may be the ultimate kernel of my being, which created and evolved this whole thing (my being, that is to say). It was impossible for me not to suppose, therefore, that this consciousness implied a duty, and that even if I were only postulating this duty, its commandments were nevertheless inviolable or, to be more accurate, they could, of course, be violated, but only with the feeling that one has violated the commandment, in other words with a guilty conscience; yet at the same time, and as far as I am concerned, this is the most peculiar part of it, this commandment is not exclusively—how shall I put it?—a moral commandment; no, it also contains an element, requirement, indeed demand, calling directly on one's handcrafting talents, so to say, that the world "must be constructed," "must be described," "must be studied," and at a time of its own choosing one must be able to demonstrate—it doesn't matter why, it doesn't matter to whom: to anybody who will be ashamed on our account and (possibly) for us—that one's religious duty, totally independently of the crippling religions of crippling churches, is therefore *understanding* the world; yes, that when all is said and done, it is in this, in understanding the world and my situation, and in this alone, that I may seek my—and again, how shall I put it in order not to say what I am bound to say?—my salvation; yes, for what else would I seek, if I am already seeking something, were it not my salvation? Then again, I also supposed that all this is merely the sort of thought that one is bound to think; in other words, that a person thinks these sorts of thoughts as a result of his condition, because he is compelled to think these sorts of thoughts as a consequence of his condition, and since a person's condition, at least in certain respects, is a condition that is prescribed and predetermined from the outset, a person is therefore able to think solely predetermined thoughts, or at least ruminate and ponder solely on matters, subjects and problems that are prescribed and predetermined from the outset. For this reason, I supposed, I ought to be thinking thoughts that I don't *have to* think, but I no longer recollect if, after that, I did indeed ponder on such thoughts, apart from pondering at all, of course, which I didn't *have to* do, and becoming a writer and literary translator, which there was all the less reason for me to *have to* become, indeed, which I was only able to become in spite of circumstances, by outwitting and deceiving circumstances, by incessantly hiding away and escaping into the labyrinth of circumstances, out of the path of the bullheaded monster whose galloping feet, only in passing as it were, trampled on me now and then, even so, in spite of the monstrous and devastating circumstances, which did not brook thought in any form except in the form of slave thoughts, which is to say not at all; circumstances which glorified, exalted and celebrated slave labor alone and under which I was able to live, be and exist at all practically only in secret, by denying myself out loud and shielding fearfully and mutely within myself my velvety-black night and hopeless hope, which perhaps first slipped past my lips, many, many, many years later, that evening when—taking note, from time to time, of a woman's gaze that was fixed on me as if seeking to tap a source from within me—I spoke about "Teacher," that there is a pure concept, untrammeled by any foreign material, whether our body, our soul, our wild beasts, a notion which lives as a uniform image in all our minds, yes, an ideal which (and I did not say this, though I secretly thought it), which perhaps I too will be able to stalk, get closer to and one day even succeed in capturing in writing, a thought that I suppose I don't *have to* think but think independently of myself, as it were, and think even if the thought speaks against me, even if it annihilates me, indeed perhaps truly then, because that is perhaps how I would recognize it, that may perhaps be the measure of the thought . . . Yes, so that was the way I was living at that time. And now that I am relating all this, I do indeed roughly understand and recognize what I need to understand and recognize. As to whether this moment might have differed from other, similar or not even the slightest bit similar moments of mine that initiated a relationship or affair, I can only answer: yes, indeed, it differed radically from them. Just as, at least in a certain sense, I myself also differed radically from myself. For to sum up my subtenant life at that time, my thoughts, my inclinations, my motives, my whole subtenanted survival state at that time, I have to conclude that all the signs are that already then everything stood ripe and ready within me for a *change of state*. I am surely not imagining it when I suppose that I started to speculate, mistakenly, and thus untenably and intolerably, about my life. That I should not look on my life merely as a series of arbitrary accidents succeeding the arbitrary accident of my birth, because that was not just an unworthy, mistaken, and thus untenable, indeed intolerable, but above all, *useless*—at least for me, an intolerably and shamefully useless—view of life, which I ought to and wish to see much rather as a series of flashes of recognition in which my pride, at least my pride, can take satisfaction. Consequently, the moment in which it was decided that I would soon be going to bed with a woman, that is, *with her*, who was to became my wife and later my ex-wife, that moment could not have been an accidental moment either. Because it is absolutely clear that everything I have written down here, and which, as I said, stood ripe and ready within me for a *change of state* was now, as it were, summed up in this moment, even though by the nature of things, I myself could not have been aware of it as yet, yes, even though all I can recollect is her face upraised towards me in the dancing lights of the night, soft-grained and at the same time glassily opalescent and glistening, like a 1930s close-up. Who would have believed where and what I would be enticed to by the promising gleam of this face. And if I add that, as it later became clear, everything likewise stood ripe and ready for a *change of state* within her too, my future (or ex-) wife, then I may also submit that our meeting was not only not accidental but manifestly a fated meeting. Yes, not much time passed before we were talking about our shared life, though in reality we wanted a fate, both of us our own fate, since that is always individual, unlike anybody else's, and cannot be shared with anybody else's. Whatever we talked about, therefore, was all just talking beside the point, pretext and equivocation, albeit undoubtedly not *deliberate* talking beside the point, pretext and equivocation, or in other words, not lying. Because how could I have known, as today I know better than all else, that everything I do and which happens to me, that my states and occasional changes in state, altogether my entire life—my godfathers!—serve for me merely as means to recognition in the series of my flashes of recognition—my marriage, for instance, serving as a means towards the recognition that I am unable to live in a married state. And *decisive* as this recognition was in the series of my flashes of recognition, it was just as *fateful*, of course, from the viewpoint of my marriage, even if, from other points of view, coldly considered, without marrying I could never have reached this recognition, or at best could only have reached it through abstract inferences. Thus, there seems to be no escaping every accusation and self-accusation, the sole excuse that I have going for me being identical to the accusation that can be leveled against me: that when I contracted my marriage, which as I now see was undoubtedly out of motives and for the aim of self-liquidation, it was at least my belief that I was, on the contrary, contracting it under the badge of the future, of happiness, that happiness about which my wife and I had spoken so much and so timidly, yet also intimately and resolutely, as if it were some secret and almost grim duty that had been sternly laid upon us. Yes, that's how it was, and now our entire life, its every sound, incident and feeling, is something I see, or rather, however strange, hear, like some kind of musical fabric beneath which the main, great, all-embracing, one-and-only theme continually ripens and condenses in order that, bursting out and outblasting all else, it may assume its autocracy: *my existence viewed as the potentiality of your being*, and later: *your non-existence viewed as the necessary and radical liquidation of my own existence*. It was just a pretext that straightaway that evening, in talking about "Teacher," continuing with the lessons of "Teacher's" case, or more specifically his act, I laid bare and explained to my wife (who at that time was not yet and is now no longer my wife), as I say, I enlightened her as to the chances, or rather lack of chances, of deeds that are doable in such situations, that is, in situations of totalitarianism. Because, I said, totalitarianism is a mindless situation, hence each and every situation that supervenes within it is also a mindless situation, although, I said, and perhaps this is the most mindless aspect of it all, by very virtue of our lives, merely by sustaining our lives, we ourselves contribute to sustaining totalitarianism, of course insofar as we insist, I said, on sustaining our lives; and this is merely, as it were, a self-fulfilling, one might almost say primitive trick of organization, I said. Hypotheses of totalitarianism are, so to say, naturally based on Nothingness, I said. Selection and expulsion as well as the notions on which they are based, are all nonexistent, null and void notions, I said, and they have no other reality than their sheer naturalism—for instance, shoving a person into a gas chamber, I said. I fear all this could not have been too entertaining, and if I now reflect on whether there might have been some other aim to what I said, beyond what I said, to the best of my recollection there was not; as best I recollect it was just my anguish still speaking out of me, the same compulsion to speak that had also made me speak a few hours earlier at the gathering, as well as my impression, however odd or unusual it may have been, that the woman who was walking beside me, walking beside me on her clacking high-heeled shoes, and thus whom I could see only vaguely, from the side and in the gloom of the night, though I did not even try to look at her because I still carried within me the image of her as, barely an hour before, she had traversed a greenish-blue carpet towards me as if she were making her way on the sea, and thus this woman walking by my side was *interested* in what I was saying. In totalitarianism, I said, executioners and victims alike perform a total service in a single cause, the cause of Nothingness, though naturally, I said, that service is *by no means an identical* service. And although "Teacher's" act was an act performed under totalitarianism, an act extorted by totalitarianism, and hence ultimately an act of totalitarianism, or in other words of mindlessness, the act itself was nevertheless an act of total victory over total mindlessness, precisely because only here, in a world of total termination and extermination, could the ineradicability of the ideal—or obsession, if you prefer—that was alive within "Teacher" transfigure into a *declaration*. She then asked whether, apart from what I had been made to suffer, I had suffered or was maybe still suffering perhaps from my Jewishness as such. I replied that I would have to think about that. There is no denying that I have known and felt since long ago, from the first stirrings of my thoughts, that some mysterious shame is attached to my name, and that I brought this shame with me from some place where I had never been, and I brought it on account of some sin, which, even though I never committed it, is my sin and will pursue me throughout my life, a life which is undoubtedly not my own life, even though it is me who is living it, me who suffers from it, and me who will later die from it; nevertheless, I suppose all of that, I said to my wife, does not necessarily have to ensue from my Jewishness, it may simply ensue from me, from my essence, my person, my transcendental self, if I may put it that way, or else from the general and reciprocal modes of behavior and manners of treatment shown towards me and practiced by me, or in plain language from the social conditions and my personal relationship to those conditions, I said, for as it has been written *judgment does not come suddenly, the proceedings gradually merge into the judgment*, I said. The subject of my "piece" came up as well, the particular piece of writing that she had read and which, as she said, she *absolutely* had to discuss with me. Which means that I too must speak about this particular piece of writing, to give a broad outline of what sort of piece it was. The piece was, in point of fact, an extended short story of the type that is usually described as a "novella," which had been published around that time deep within the haystack of a bulky anthology of short stories and novellas, by no means without all sorts of denigrating and insulting precursory complications that I shall refrain from describing, because they bore and disgust me, besides which, in itself, it was merely a modest and, one could say, dispensable contribution to Hungarian literary life, that denigrating and insulting, and, above all else, shameless and shameful literary life, resting as it does on its exclusions, privileges, pre- and postdilections, its official and confidential commercial blacklisting systems always casting doubt on quality, always unctuously deferential to aggressive dilettantism as if it were genius, of which I was, and am, a now horrified, now astonished, now indifferent, but always merely external observer, insofar as I am and must be at all—oh, what do I have to do with literature, with your golden hair, Margarethe, for a ballpoint pen is my spade, the sepulchre of your ashen hair, Shulamith; yes, anyway, this short story or novella, so be it, is a monologue by a man, a man still on the youngish side. This man, who had been brought up by his parents in the strictest Christian faith, or bigotry, one might say, now finds out, during the days of the apocalypse, that the unsealed brand has been placed on him too: *in the spirit* of the so-called laws that suddenly come into force, he is classed as a Jew. Now, before they take him away to the ghetto, the cattle wagon, or to who knows (he least of all) where and what sort of death they will condemn him, he writes his story, "the story of decades of cowardice and self-denial," as he writes (that is to say, I have him write). Now, what is noteworthy about the whole thing is that in his brand-new Jewish existence he finds a release from his Jewish complex, a general liberation, for he has to recognize that merely being debarred from one community does not automatically make one a member of another. "What do I have to do with the Jews?" he asks (that is to say, I make him ask): nothing, he realizes (that is, I make him realize), now that he is one himself. While he had been enjoying the privileges of a non-Jewish existence he had suffered on account of Jews, or Jewish existence or, to be more precise, the whole corrupt, suffocating, deadly and death-dealing suicidal system of privileges and discriminations. He had suffered on account of some of his friends, colleagues at the office, the wider community at large that he believed was his *homeland*; he had suffered from their hatred, their narrow-mindedness, their fanaticism. He had conceived a particular abhorrence for the inescapable debates that went on about anti-Semitism, the excruciating futility of all those debates, as if anti-Semitism, he realizes (that is, I make him realize), were not a matter of conviction but of temperament and character, "the morality of despair, the frenzy of self-haters, the vitality of devastators," as he says (that is, I have him say). On the other hand, he had also felt a certain awkwardness towards Jews in that, try as he might to like them, he was never sure about the success of the attempt. He had Jewish acquaintances, even friends, whom he either liked or disliked; yet that was different, because he had liked or disliked them out of purely individual considerations or reasons. But how could one feel an active liking for an abstract notion like the notion of Jewishness, for example? Or for the unknown mass of people that was crammed into this abstract notion? To the extent that he succeeded, he succeeded somehow only by dint of liking them the way one likes a stray animal that one has to feed but about which one has no way of telling what it is dreaming and what it is capable of. Now he was relieved of this torment, his entire presumed responsibility. With a clear conscience he could now despise whomever he despised, and he no longer had to like those whom he disliked. He is liberated because he no longer has a homeland. All he has to decide is what he should die as. As a Jew or a Christian, as a hero or victim, possibly as the injured party of a metaphysical absurdity or of a demiurgic neochaos? Since these concepts mean nothing to him, he decides that at least he will not pollute the pure fact of his death with lies. He sees everything simply because he has won the right to clear-sightedness: "We should not seek meaning where there is none: the century, this execution squad on permanent duty, is now once again preparing for decimation, and destiny has decreed that one of the tenth lots should be cast on me—that's all there is to it," are the last words he says (with my own words, of course). Of course, it wasn't all quite so spare, but here I have stripped it down to the essentials, leaving out the dialogues, the twists in the plot, the setting and the other characters, including that of the lover who leaves him. The last time we see our hero he is seated on the ground, rocking to and fro, bursting in an uncontrollable fit of laughter. "The Laugh" was indeed what I had intended to use as the title, but the director of the publishing house, who was widely known to carry a *service weapon* at all times, even in his office (the publishing house), even though he was never to be seen in uniform and he did not even carry this *service weapon*, an automatic, in a service holster but tucked into a bulging hip pocket of his trousers; well anyway, this *director* rejected the title as being "cynical" and "trampling on the sanctity of memories," and so forth, so how the story came to be published at all, albeit with a disfigured title, is something I have never understood to the present day, nor do I wish to understand, because I am repelled that I might understand and gain a glimpse into the inextricable web of ulterior motives which spares nothing at all, destroys everything, and even what it does allow to exist, it does so only for destructive motives; so, just like the figure I created, I too content myself with the fact that in the course of the decimation—though it was much more like a trisection—my story, somehow or other, happened to draw one of the lucky numbers. What had gripped my wife in the story was, as she put it, that *a person can decide for himself about his Jewishness*. Until then, whenever she had read works about Jews or concerning Jews she had felt as if she was *once again having her face ground into the mud*. Now, for the first time, my wife said, she felt that *she could hold her head high*. On reading my piece, my wife said, she had felt what my "hero" had felt, for although he dies, before that *he is accorded inner liberation*. Even if only fleetingly, she too had experienced that sense of liberation, my wife said. More than anything before, this piece of writing *taught her how to live*, my wife said, and for the second time that evening the swiftly alternating ripple of expressions again flickered across her face, that—I don't know how else to put it—chromaticism of smiles which gave me the feeling I could melt and be transformed into anything. I soon became acquainted with the background to these statements, my wife's childhood and adolescence. Although my wife had been born after Auschwitz, childhood and adolescence had been spent under the mark of Auschwitz. More specifically, under the mark of being Jewish. Under the mark of the mud, to quote from my wife's aforementioned words. My wife's parents had both passed through Auschwitz: I was still able to make the acquaintance of her father, a tall, bald-headed man, with features that were guardedly austere in the presence of strangers but unreservedly harsh in the circle of his more intimate friends or family, but she had lost her mother early on. The woman had died of some disease brought back from Auschwitz, sometimes swelling up and at other times losing weight, sometimes suffering bouts of colic and at other times covered with skin eruptions, a disease that science proved effectively powerless to tackle, just as science also proved effectively powerless to tackle the precipitating cause of the disease, Auschwitz, for the disease my wife's mother had suffered from was, in reality, Auschwitz itself, and there is no cure for Auschwitz, nobody will ever recover from the disease of Auschwitz. Her mother's illness and early death had incidentally played a decisive part in determining that my wife should become a physician, my wife said. Later on, while talking about such matters, my wife cited a couple of sentences which, she said, she no longer knew where she had read but she had never forgotten since. Not immediately, but quite soon afterwards, it occurred to me that my wife must have read the sentences in one of the essays of *Untimely Meditations*, the one entitled "On the Uses and Disadvantages of History for Life," and this reinforced my belief that the sentences we have a need for seek us out sooner or later, because if I didn't believe that, I don't understand how those sentences could have reached my wife, who, to the best of my knowledge, never showed any interest in philosophy, least of all in Nietzsche. The exact sentences, which I soon tracked down in the disintegrating, red-bound volume of Nietzsche that I had seized upon once in some dark corner of an antiquarian bookseller's, read as follows, albeit not in my own translation: *There is a degree of sleeplessness, of rumination, of the historical sense, which is harmful and ultimately fatal to the living thing, whether this living thing be a man or a people or a culture.* After which, or before it, I couldn't say offhand: . . . *He who cannot sink on the threshold of the moment and forget all the past, who cannot stand balanced like a goddess of victory without growing dizzy and afraid*—and from here on my wife knew it by heart—*will never know what happiness is—worse, he will never do anything to make others happy*. My wife was made aware of her Jewishness, and all that was bound up with this, in early childhood. There had been a time—"my ponytailed, freckle-faced little-girl period," my wife called it—when she had imagined that *the other children would have to love her a lot* on account of all that. Now that I come to write down her words, I suddenly see her, the way she laughed when she said that. Later on her Jewishness became equated for her with a sense of futility. With defeatism, despondency, suspicion, insidious fear, her mother's illness. Among strangers a dark secret, at home a ghetto of *Jewish feelings, Jewish thoughts*.

After her mother died, an aunt of her father had moved in with them. "She has such an Auschwitz look," she had immediately thought, my wife said. Seeing only a former or future murderer in everybody. "I don't know how I still managed to grow up into a more or less healthy woman." Leaving the room the moment that *Jewish matters* were mentioned. "Something turned to stone inside me and resisted." Hardly spending any time at home. Studying was an escape as later on were medicine and lovers, several brief and passionate affairs. She had had two "most awful experiences," my wife said—both, she remembered, when she was around sixteen or seventeen years old. On one occasion she had spoken heatedly about the French Revolution, saying it had been little better than the Nazis. Her great-aunt responded by saying that she, being a Jew, had no right to talk about the French Revolution in that way, because had there been no French Revolution the Jews would still be living in ghettos today. After this rebuke from the great-aunt, so my wife remembered, she had not spoken a word at home for days or maybe even weeks. She had felt that she herself no longer existed, that she had no right at all to lay claim to her own feelings or thoughts, that solely because she had been born a Jew she could have only *Jewish feelings* and *Jewish thoughts*. That was when *every day they ground her face into the mud* had been formulated and she had declared it to herself for the first time. The second experience: she is sitting with a book in her hand, a book about atrocities, with photographs of atrocities, a vacantly staring, bespectacled face behind barbed wire, a young boy with a yellow star, hands raised in the air, his peakless cap slipping down over his eyes, on either side an escort of armed soldiers; she is looking at these pictures and a cold chill of malice, from she herself takes fright, creeps into her heart, and exactly the same thought occurs to her as my "hero" had thought in my short story: "What has this to do with me? I'm a Jew myself," my wife said. But until she had read these and other similar thoughts in my story, she had only been able to think them uneasily, and afterwards had felt guilty for having them. That was why, after reading my story, my wife said, she had felt *she could hold her head high*. And she repeated, and more than once at that, that I *taught her how to live*: that beside me, my wife said, she felt herself to be *free*. Yes, in this dark and all-illuminating night of mine these are the sounds, images and motifs that now stand out from the jumble of those few lightning-fast years that were my marriage, until I suddenly see ourselves at a window, the window of our apartment, again at night time, a no-longer-winter-but-not-yet-spring evening when the city's noxious vapors were pervaded now and again by a scent that came, like an otherworldly message, perhaps from distant plants that were stirring anew, out of habit as it were, seeking to live anew, out of habit as it were, and on the other side of the road three half-drunk men were stumbling homewards from the nearby bar, the white fur collar on the sheepskin coat one of them was wearing gleamed up towards our window and, holding on to each other, they were singing in subdued voices, the last traffic in the street had just sped by, there was a moment's silence, then, as in an orchestral pause, their voices too carried up to us, and we could hear clearly what they were singing: *We've just come from Auschwitz, there's more of us than before*, the sound drifted up into the night, and at first I did not actually hear it, but then I did hear it. But what does it have to do with me, I thought, so-called anti-Semitism is a purely private affair that, even though I personally may die from it anywhere, at any time, even today, after Auschwitz, I reflected, nowadays that would be a sheer anachronism, a fallacy in which, as H. would say, not H., Leader and Chancellor, but H., philosopher and head butler to all leaders and chancellors, the *World-Spirit* is no longer present, in other words, a provincialism, nothing more, a genius loci, a local idiocy; and if they want to shoot or beat me to death, I reflected, they will say so in good time, I reflected, the way they have generally always given prior notice. Only then did I look at my wife, cautiously, because she was suspiciously quiet, and in the cold light from the street and the warmer light that was filtering out from the room behind us I clearly saw the tears streaming down her face. There will never be an end to it, my wife said, there is no escaping this curse, she said, and if only she knew what it was that made her a Jew, given that she was simply incapable of religious faith and, possibly out of laziness or cowardice, or as a result of other predilections, she was simply unacquainted with the specifically Jewish culture of the Jews, and also incapable of showing any interest in it as it simply did not interest her, she said, so what was it that made her Jewish, if in fact neither language, nor lifestyle, nothing, nothing at all, singled her out from others who lived around her, unless, she said, it was some sort of occult, atavistic message hidden away in the genes that she herself did not hear and therefore could not know about. At which point, dispassionately, callously, and almost calculatedly, as with a well-directed dagger thrust or a sudden strong embrace, I told her that was all a waste of time, her searching for presumed causes and pseudo-explanations was futile, just one thing made her Jewish, nothing else: *The fact that you were* not *in Auschwitz,* I told her, and at this my wife fell silent, first like a scared child, but then the features very quickly changed back into her own, the features of the wife I knew and of someone else whom I only now discovered in my wife's familiar face, a discovery which, so to speak, shook me; and our by then not so torrid nights were rekindled once again. Because, yes, by then the contradictions in my marriage were already starting to show, or to be accurate, my marriage had begun to show itself for what it was: a contradiction. In recollecting those times, I recall most of all certain reflexes of mine which kept me in a state of constant tension and internal agitation, in much the same way, perhaps—at least this is how I imagine it—as beavers, those actually rodent-like small creatures, must be driven by instinct to construct and model their complicated systems, veritable strongholds, of dams, escape passages and chambers. Around that time, besides of course literary translation, the stacks of translations that enabled me to put bread on the table, I was preoccupied by a plan for a more ambitious literary work; a novel, the subject of which, skipping the details here, was to be a soul's path, the path of a striving from darkness to light, a struggle to attain joy, engagement in this struggle as an obligation, *happiness viewed as a duty.* At that time I talked a great deal (no, that is an understatement: at that time I talked almost incessantly) about this plan with my wife, who visibly took the greatest possible pleasure in these discussions, and above all in my plan as such, because in it she saw, and of course not entirely without reason, a monument to our marriage as it were, and therefore I could never tell her enough about it, describing the plot, sketchy at first, of course, but later plumped out from day to day, the proliferating and solidifying and ramifying motifs and ideas, to which, amid a flicker of chromatics suddenly brightening then swiftly fading across her face, she would attach her own timorous comments, to which every now and again, and precisely in hope of that chromaticism of the play of features, I would give approving assent, encouragement and appreciation; we raised this plan together, so to speak, nursing and coddling and petting it as if it were our own child. Looking back, of course, it was all a mistake, no doubt, a mistake to allow my wife to encroach upon this most sensitive, most secret, most unprotected sanctum of my life, my existence, which in a word is my *work*, a sanctum that, quite to the contrary, I have to protect and defend, as I had done before and have done ever since, so to say surrounding it with a barbed-wire fence against all unauthorized intruders, against the very possibility of intrusion, any sort of intrusion, by anybody; just as it is an indisputable fact that I did indeed sense the danger in the intense interest on my wife's part, embracing and reaching into my whole life, fierce and yet at the same time achingly tender, while on the other hand, I did not in all honesty wish to forgo that interest either, just as one does not wish to forgo the warming sunshine that suddenly bursts upon one after the long dark days of winter. For when it came to my setting out to realize my plan, to actually write the novel, it turned out that the concept was unrealizable; it turned out that the material oozing from my ballpoint pen, as from an infective pustule, into the entire tissue of the plan, each and every cell of it, was such, I would say, as to pathologically alter that tissue, each and every cell of it; it turned out that it is impossible to write about happiness, or at least I can't, which in this case amounts to the same thing after all; happiness is perhaps too simple to let itself be written about, I wrote, as I am reading right now on a slip of paper that I wrote then and from which I am writing it down here; a life lived in happiness is therefore a life lived in muteness, I wrote. It turned out that writing about life amounts to thinking about life, and thinking about life amounts to casting doubt on life, but only one who is suffocated by his very lifeblood, or in whom it somehow circulates unnaturally, casts doubt on that lifeblood. It turned out that I don't write in order to seek pleasure; on the contrary, it turned out that by writing I am seeking pain, the most acute possible, well-nigh intolerable pain, most likely because pain is truth, and as to what constitutes truth, I wrote, the answer is so simple: truth is what consumes you, I wrote. Naturally, I could impart none of this to my wife. On the other hand, I did not want to lie to my wife either. As a result, therefore, we came up against certain difficulties in the course of our time together and our discussions, especially when the subject of my work, and most especially the *achievements* that could be expected from my work, was brought up: writing as *literature*, the to me remote, unimportant and infinitely uninteresting issue of likes or dislikes, the question of the *meaning* of my work, questions that, in the end, mostly debouched into the shameful, squalid, insulting and humiliating topic of success or the lack of it. How could I have explained to my wife that my ballpoint pen is my spade? That I write only because I have to write, and I have to write because I am whistled up every day to drive the spade deeper, to play death on a darker, sweeter string? How could I be expected to complete my self-liquidation, my sole business on this earth, while fostering within myself some seductive ulterior motive, the seductive ulterior motive of *achievement*, *literature*, or maybe *success*?

How could my wife, or anyone else, wish for me to *put to use* my spectacular self-liquidation and, what is more, put it to use so that I might thereby sneak, like a thief with a skeleton key, into some sort of literary or other future from which I have already been debarred by reason of my birth, and from which I have anyway debarred myself, and to accomplish work founded on that future with the selfsame strokes of the grubbing hoe with which I must dig my grave bed in the clouds, the winds, the nothingness? It is questionable whether I myself saw my position as clearly, as distinctly, as I am now describing it. Perhaps not completely, but the aspiration, not to speak of the good intention, was undeniably there within me. As to what I might have been thinking then, and with what sorts of feelings I might have been grappling, a good indication is given by a fragmentary slip of paper that I found when searching through the fragments of my marriage. Evidently, it was a slip that I had intended to place beside my wife's tea cup, as I was accustomed to doing at times when, due to *my work* having stretched late into the night, I did not get up for breakfast. This is what it says: ". . . That we should be able to love one another and yet still remain *free*, though I am well aware neither of us is able to evade the lot of a man and the lot of a woman, and thus we shall be party to this torment that a mysterious and, in truth, none too wise Nature has apportioned to us; in other words, that the time will come again when I shall reach out my hand for you and desire you, and all I shall desire is that you be mine; yet at the same time as you too reach out your hand and finally become mine, I shall still place bounds on you in your submission in order that I may preserve what I imagine to be *my freedom* . . ." So much for the fragment, and since I found it among my writings, a slip of paper mixed up among my other slips of paper, it is certain that I did not prop it up against my wife's tea cup but must somehow have mixed it up together with my writings and slips of paper, but it is also certain that is secretly what I thought, and I lived in accordance with my thoughts, indeed directly lived those thoughts, inasmuch as *I always did have a secret life, and that was always my real life.* Yes, it was around then that I started to construct my escape passages, my beaver stronghold, to hide and shield things away from my wife's eyes and hands, so that from time to time—and, I have no doubt, on account of my defensive barriers—I fancied that I detected a lurking resentment in my wife's behavior, and this observation grew into a reciprocal resentment and later into a persistent anguish within me that portrayed, or sought to portray, my wife's shifting mood as a much more serious resentment than it really was, since it would not have taken much effort on my part to appease my wife, little more than a single appropriate, timely and well-chosen word, even one such gesture, would have done the trick, yet I clung to my anguish, obviously because I perceived my state of rejection in it, while the intolerable feeling of rejection sought compensation, and lonely compensation in turn manifested itself within me once again as creative force; in other words, it ignited my neurosis, my love of work, my fever and rage for work, haughtily carrying all before it but only necessitating newer and still more strenuous defensive reflexes, in short, re-activating the whole diabolical mechanism, the deadly merry-go-around, which first dips me in my anguish only to raise me aloft, but solely in order to quickly hurl me back, ever deeper . . . And certainly, quite certainly, this too played a part in the rekindling of our nights, on one of which darkly glittering nights, whose dark, velvety light nevertheless differed so much from the dark, black lights that lose themselves in the darkness of my present night—on one of our darkly glowing nights my wife said that to all of our questions and answers, those questions and answers that touch upon our entire life, we can only respond with our lives as a whole, or to be more precise, with our entire lives, because every question we pose from now on and every answer we give from now on would be an unsatisfactory question and an unsatisfactory answer, and she could imagine fulfillment only one way, because, for her at least, no other fulfillment could substitute for that sole, undivided, genuine fulfillment, or in other words, she wanted a child by me, my wife said. Yes, and

"No!" I said instantly and at once, without hesitation and virtually instinctively as it has become quite natural by now that our instincts should act contrary to our instincts, that our counterinstincts, so to say, should act instead of, indeed as, our instincts; and my wife just laughed, as if that

"No!" had not been a decisive enough

"No!" or as if she had been sure of my inconsistency. She understood me, she said later, she knew what depths that

"No!" must have burst forth from within me, and what I would have to subjugate within myself for it to become a *yes*. I responded that I believed I in turn understood her, what she was thinking, but the

"No!" was a

"No!" and not the sort of *Jewish no* that she was probably

thinking; no, I was quite sure about that, as sure as I was unsure about exactly what kind of a

"No!" it was, it was just a

"No!" I said, though as far as a *Jewish no* is concerned, there would be justification enough for that, too, since it was enough to imagine a distressing and shameful conversation, I said, let's say, I said, to imagine a child's cry, our child's (your) screaming, let's say, I said; the child has heard something and just happens to be screaming, "I don't want to be a Jew!" let's say, I said, since it is very easy to imagine and easy to justify, I said, that the child may not want to be a Jew, let's say, and I would be hard put to respond to that; yes, because how can one compel a living being to be a Jew, in this respect, I said, I would have to go about with my head hung low before it (before you), because there is nothing I could give it (you), no explanation, no belief, no ammunition, since my own Jewishness means nothing to me, or to be more precise, in terms of its Jewishness nothing, in terms of the experience everything, as Jewishness: a bald-headed woman in a red negligee in front of the mirror, as experience: my life, my survival, the cerebral mode of existence that I live and maintain as a cerebral mode of existence, and for me that is sufficient, I am perfectly satisfied with that much; it is questionable, however, if it (you) would be satisfied with that much. And yet, I said, I am not saying a *Jewish no*, despite everything, because there is nothing more abominable, more shameful, more destructive and more self-repudiating than this kind of, so to say, rational *no*, this kind of *Jewish no*, there is nothing tawdrier than that, nothing more cowardly, I said, I have had enough of murderers and deniers of life proclaiming themselves to be for life, it happens far too often, I said, for it to rouse in me even so much as a rebellious squeak of defiance, there is nothing more appalling, more disgraceful than to deny life for the sake of the deniers of life, for children were born even in Auschwitz, I said, and not unnaturally this line of reasoning appealed to my wife, though I find it hard to believe she could really have understood, any more than probably I myself really understood. Yes, and it cannot have been long after this that I had to take a tramcar, to go who knows where, obviously going about my business, as if I still had any business now that all my earthly business has already been accomplished, and I was gazing out of the window during the rickety trundling, the unexpected halts at tram stops. We clattered along past frightful houses and the faint shrieks of sporadic scatterings of stunted vegetation and all at once, as in an onslaught, a family alighted. I forgot to mention that it was a Sunday, a discreetly dwindling Sunday afternoon going into the warmer time of year. There were five of them, the parents and three daughters. The youngest, barely out of swaddling clothes and resplendent in pink, blue and blonde, was dribbling and screaming tenaciously, perhaps because she was too hot, I thought. The mother, brunette, placid, exhausted, took her on her lap, her slender neck crooked over the infant in the semiarched pose of a ballerina at the opera. The middle sister stood sulking beside her mother as the latter cuddled the youngest, while the eldest girl, who I supposed was seven or eight years old, so to say in a gesture of conciliation and the wretched fellowship of outcasts, laced her arm around her younger sister's shoulder but was peevishly shrugged off. The middle sister wanted her mother to herself but knew this was a forlorn cause, as was her weapon, the unbridled screaming that had now become the prerogative of the youngest. The eldest girl was now on her own; that pleasantly lit Sunday afternoon she was again experiencing the bitter pill of being ignored, loneliness and jealousy. Would that mature within her into a welcoming forgiveness, I wondered, or rather into a hide-in-the-corner neurosis, I wondered, while her father and mother browbeat her into some sort of shameful existence, I wondered, to which she will reconcile herself, I wondered, and comply shamefacedly, or if not shamefacedly, all the more shame on her and on all those who browbeat and reconciled her to that, I wondered. The father, a wiry, brown-haired, bespectacled man in summery linen shorts, sandals on his bare feet, Adam's apple like a goiter, stretched out his jaundiced bony hand, the infant finally calmed down between his knobbly knees; and suddenly, like a transcendental message, an overarching similarity broke out on the five faces. They were ugly, harrowed, pitiful and beatific, within me vied mixed feelings of revulsion and attraction, horrific memories and melancholy, and written on their foreheads, so to say, as well as on the sides of the tramcar I saw in flaming letters a:

"No!" I could never be another person's father, destiny, god,

"No!" what happened to me, my childhood, must never happen to another child,

"No!" something screamed and whined within me, it is impossible that this, childhood, should happen to it (to you) and to me; yes, and that was when I started to tell the story of my childhood to my wife, or maybe it was to myself, I don't rightly know, but I told the story with the full prodigality and compulsiveness of my logorrhea, told it unrestrainedly for days and weeks on end, as a matter of fact I am still telling the story now, though since long ago not to my wife. Yes, and not only to tell the story, for around that time I also started to roam about, and the selfsame city in which I had been going about in the relative security of relative habit now began, around that time, to turn again into a trap for me and periodically open up beneath my feet, so I could never know upon which unspeakable location, pervaded with agonies and ignominies, I might unexpectedly stumble, or what summons I was yielding to, for instance, when I would sneak into a side street, dozing like some illustrious patient between the tiny, crippled, dream-wreck palaces, or steal between the shadows of turreted, weather-cocked, lace-curtained, steeply gabled, blind-windowed fairy-tale houses, along the black railings of vile front gardens in which everything was now as ransacked, as bare, brazen, shoddy and rational as a deserted excavation site. Or, on yet another occasion, how I ended up in the—how can I put it?—entrails of the city, to which, by the way, I have come back again as a resident, through a twist of fate, if you like, or through ineptitude, if you like that better, but let's rather say through a twist of fate, now it makes no difference and inasmuch as one may detect one's fate even in one's ineptitude, if one has the eye for it; yes, maybe at that time I believed (or, to be more precise, deluded myself) that I had fetched up here inadvertently, in the selfsame place, the bowels of the Józsefváros city district, where they abut the bowels of the Ferencváros district, that is to say roughly where I still live today, though the prefabricated apartment of my prefabricated tower block could then only have been a misbegotten draft on a misbegotten blueprint. It was a dusk towards the end of summer, I remember, the street suffused with overripe smells, its small-windowed houses tottering squint-eyed, tipsy and unwashed along the sidewalks, the sinking sun pouring like yellow, sticky, fermenting grape must all across their walls, the gates murkily yawning like scabs of impetigo, and, feeling dizzy, I clung to a door knob, or who knows what, as I was suddenly grazed by—oh, certainly not by a sense of transience, on the contrary, by the *mystery of continuance*; yes, a murderer must feel this, I supposed then later told my wife, and why I should happen to have supposed that of all things may not, I suppose be logical but is understandable, I must have supposed it on account of the dead, I suppose, I told my wife, on account of my dead, my dead childhood and my absurd—at any rate absurd when set against my dead and my dead childhood—survival; yes, a murderer must feel this way if, let's say, I supposed and later told my wife, having long forgotten his deed (which is conceivable, nor is it such a rarity at that) decades later, let's say out of forgetfulness or maybe just by mechanically reproducing his former habits, suddenly happens to reopen the door on the scene of the crime, and he finds everything there unchanged: the corpse, though it has decomposed by now into a skeleton, the tawdry props of the furniture, not forgetting himself, and no matter how obvious it is that by now nothing and nobody is the same as it or he was, it's just as obvious that after the brief interlude of a generation everything is nevertheless exactly the same as it was, *indeed even more so*. And now he knows what he needs to know, that it was *by no means* chance that led him back, indeed, that perhaps he never even got out of there, because *this is the place where he must atone.* And don't ask, I said to my wife, why he must, because crime and atonement are concepts between which only being brings a living link into being, if it brings anything into being of course, and if it has already brought something into being, then being in itself is quite enough to qualify as a crime, *el delito mayor del hombre es haber nacido*, somebody wrote,* I said to my wife. I also told my wife about one of my dreams, a recurrent old dream that I had not dreamed for quite some time but which had unexpectedly come back again in those days. It takes place there, yes, always *there*, on that spot, in that corner house. I can't see the neighborhood, it's true, but I know this for sure. It may be that the walls permit that conclusion, the thick, ghostly-grey walls of a decrepit house. Along with the tobacconist's, with a flight of steep, uneven steps leading up to it. At the top it was as if one were opening the door on a rat hole: decaying gloom and a putrefying stench. But on this occasion the tobacconist's has been placed farther over, on the corner of the corner house. I have no reason at all to enter. I enter. This is not the tobacconist's, it's a bit more spacious, a bit brighter, much drier and warm, like an attic. There they sit, on an ancient *couch* set on the concrete floor, opposite an indeterminate source of light beams—a skylight, perhaps?—that sets the thick clouds of dust sifting down from above dancing. All the signs suggest that they have just sat *up*, whereas beforehand they could well have been lying down, waiting for my now decades-overdue visit, a visit from their uncaring *hope-butcher* of a grandson. An old couple in the dusty light, full of reproaches. So weak

*Man's greatest crime is to be born (Calderón: *Life Is a Dream*)

they hardly move. I hand over the ham that I have brought with me. They are pleased, but with an undiminished rancor. They speak, but I don't understand what they say. Grandfather bends his grey, bristly face over the ham, which he is holding in his hands, having meanwhile undone the wrapping paper. Livid cadaveric spots can clearly be seen on my grandmother's face. She complains about the eternal stabbing pains in her head, the buzzing in her ears. About being made to wait; that they have been waiting such a long, long time now. It is borne in on me how the ham is next to nothing for them. They are desperately hungry and abandoned. I make a few futile gestures, like a schoolboy trying to apologize. My heart feels as heavy as the stones of the steps. Then everything sinks, lifts and disperses like a shameful secret. Why must we live with our face perpetually turned towards some scene of shame? I noted down at the time. It was around the same time that my still-growing collection of quotations was started, a bundle of paper slips held together by a clip, which even now is lying about on my table, among the rest of my paper slips. *My friends, we had it tough when we were young: we suffered from youth itself as from a serious illness,* I read on one slip. *Families, I hate you!* I read on another. *Surrendering ourselves to childhood as a cause of death,* I read. *Already as a child . . . I often considered,* I read, *that the word domination, like domination, like the notion of domination, invariably signifies a domination of terror*, and appended to this quotation (from Thomas Bernhard), I read a remark of my own: "And the domination of terror in all cases signifies a paternal domination." After that, all I read on the slips are my own observations, such as: "The task of education, to which I could never be reconciled . . .";

"To influence someone else's dreams like a nightmare, to play a role, the paternal role, and thus a fatal role, in someone else's life is one of the true horrors, the terrifying aspect of which . . ."; "That (in my childhood and hence ever since) everything that signified myself was always a sin, whereas it was always a virtue if I acted in such a way as to deny and kill myself . . ."; "My grandmother's *mouth always had a stale taste.* Really: her breath smelled of mothballs. The reek of her Józsefváros apartment. The anachronistic reek of the Monarchy. The darkness of her apartment, like the darkness of that period, the thirties, inherited, and in the process of inheritance exacerbated into a disease. The dark furniture, the tenement block with its *outside corridors*, lives played out in front of one another, milky coffee for supper, matzos *crumbled* into a mug, the prohibition against turning the lights on, my grandfather reading the newspaper in the dark, the *alcove* in whose mysterious corners some dark, musty and deadly thought constantly seemed to be lurking. The nightly bedbug bloodbath . . ."; "I would gradually fence you in with all these stories, which you actually have nothing to do with, yet over time they would tower up around you like an insurmountable barrier . . ."; "What a misery childhood was, and how impatient I was to grow up, because I believed that grown-ups had a secret alliance, that they lived in perfect safety in their sadism-girt world . . ."; and so forth. Those mornings, I told my wife. Those rainy mornings, rainy Monday mornings, when my father took me back to the boarding school for yet another week. Every Monday morning lives on in my memory as a rainy Monday morning, which is absurd, of course, but indicative, I said to my wife. I recall that on just such a rainy Monday morning I suddenly made up my mind, dropping everything, dropping *my work*, and set off for that affluent suburb or, to be more precise, the suburb that had once been an affluent suburb, or which I remembered as a formerly affluent suburb, a neighborhood of turreted, weather-cocked, lace-curtained, steeply-gabled fairy-tale houses, where, as one of those turreted, steeply gabled, weather-cocked fairy-tale houses the boarding school was located. Folding my umbrella, that shining symbol of our earthly grotesqueness, the man who stepped into this subsiding house of my troubled torments and even more troubled pleasures must have been a slightly greying fellow of comfortably-off appearance, in a checked cloth cap, with dripping umbrella, I related to my wife that evening. Is that a triumph or a defeat? I wonder how *I* would have greeted that fellow, I joked that evening to my wife, would I have noticed him at all? If so, maybe I would have taken him for some sort of school inspector, an accomplice of the school governors, the powers in charge, I related to my wife that evening. Perhaps for a disagreeable violin teacher. Obviously, I would have noticed straightaway a certain awkwardness about him as well, something ridiculous which would immediately strike one, for instance, in the way he speaks to children in the measured, fastidious manner of a sex killer, I related to my wife. Nothing, nothing, nothing at all about this outlandish, botched figure fits the dreams that I wove about my adulthood; at most I might envy him his superiority, little suspecting how much it is merely an adult's superiority, in other words, lending the appearance of superiority to non-superiority, I said to my wife. I also wrote a few lines about the visit in my notebook, a few of which I am copying across into this notebook. "I was at the boarding school," I wrote. "It lies in ruins, like everything else, houses, lives, the world," I wrote. "A commemorative plaque on the wall utterly flabbergasted me. It says: *Here lived and wrote*, and so on. The headmaster. The Head. Fat Nat (as we boys used to call him). Who would have believed he was a scholar? Yes, general bungling passes as scholarship in this century . . . The garden in ruins, laid to waste. The boarding school converted into an apartment house. The ceremonial stairway with its broad stone balustrade that was such fun to slide down, where so many furtive events took place, most especially in the evenings, when, jostling with one's fellow boarders, one trudged upstairs to bed, and the sleepiness that settled on one's eyes like a carpet of snow, braking, stifling, muffling every sound, experience and desire (the time when I suddenly developed a high fever one evening, and Szilvási, a peasant lad some ten years older than me, carried me up in his arms, and when he asked *which dorm do you sleep in*? I was unable to reply because at the age of five I had never heard the word dormitory before and so didn't know what he meant): this stairway was, well, squalid, let's just leave it at that . . . The row of dormitories chopped up, one rental unit piggybacked on the other . . . The headmaster's apartment. The Head's rooms. The frightful, silent and silencing apartment that prompted and impelled one to go on tiptoe. In place of the gleaming brass doorknob an aluminum handle, like a triumphant kick in the backside . . . The study rooms on the mezzanine. The second-class *juniors* and the much-envied *seniors* once bent over their books here during the quiet hours of afternoon *prep*. The teacher on duty for that day supervising the devotions. The grave, awe-inspiring esotericism of algebra problems. These rooms now provide homes for several families. Family lives full of bustle, noise, savory smells . . . disintegration and decay of every rigid form. Communality as a disintegrating force, ultimately as death . . . The *basement*. The dining hall, the cooler, the games room (Ping-Pong). And above all, the assembly hall for *reports*. Entry is barred. A notice board announces: *Film club, tickets*, and so forth. Fine, then I'll just have to imagine the dining hall. It's better that way, so-called *reality* (their reality) won't get in the way. In that vast basement hall, lit by high-set windows, long parallel rows of tables spread with white tablecloths. The breakfasts! The one cherished ceremony of the day (except the meal after Saturday *report*), austere but still the stuff of fantasies. The breakfast setting at my designated place, my serviette stigmatized with a Roman 'one' in a serviette ring stigmatized with a Roman 'one': that was my number here, just like other numbers I have acquired in other places at other times (nowadays an eleven-digit number runs around as my proxy somewhere in the nooks and corners of unknown labyrinths as my shadow life, a second, enigmatic me about which I know nothing, even though I am answerable for it with my life, and what it does, or what is done to it, becomes my destiny). But this Roman 'one' was a truly stylish start, charming and auspicious, like the dawn of civilizations. Because I was the youngest boarder at the school . . . etc. We stood at our places freshly scrubbed, radiant, alert, famished. (I was always famished, all the time.) At the head of the table, a teacher; at the head of every table, a teacher. He would mumble a grace, a succinct, cautious, one might say diplomatic form of prayer. Care had to be taken that it was tied to neither the Jewish nor any of the Christian liturgies, that it should be both Jewish and Christian, to the uniform gratification of all gods. *Give us this day our daily bread,* let's say (I'm not sure, but something like that). At bedtime, on the other hand, I said my prayers in German (*Müde bin ich, geh' zur Ruh!* . . . etc.). I didn't understand a word but learned quickly and with that the soothing monotony of prayer, the duress of repetition, that singular hygiene the occasional omission of which would inflict a more severe wound on my soul than omitting to brush my teeth . . . Recalling the strong, compulsive and idiosyncratic religiosity of my childhood, which at first was essentially animistic, later associated with an all-seeing, invisible X-ray eye, though that, if I rightly recollect, was only after I was ten, when it was chiefly my father who took over *my education* . . . Onwards. The *cooler*. A dark lumber room full of insects. I was locked up in there once. I viewed it rationally. The love of solitude. The love of illness. The raptures of fever. Early signs of decadence, or just a well-founded loathing of people? To loll about alone in languid bliss in the big dormitory, watching how the sun reaches the apex of the chestnut tree standing in the garden while a cat, with its inimitable gait, curling up the tip of its tail, prowls along the indescribably adventure-packed roof opposite, with the intricate hiding places of its chimneys and turrets. The sudden cramping of guts in the evening, when what had been knotting the pit of the stomach the whole afternoon happens anyway: footsteps on the stairway, a clatter of steps in the corridor. The others. *They're coming*, I whispered wanly to myself, as if it were news of a disaster. The whole thing with the stomach cramps. It was linked to the *extra milk* in the morning, for my *anemia* . . . (The charm of the old milk bottles which, as it transpired, was just as delicate and transient as the pearls of moisture on those slim bottles with the fluted edges and closely scored smooth facets, so pleasingly bumpy to the touch.) It had to be drunk. My stomach ached for ages afterwards. The sphincter of my stomach. I would be bent double as if I had been KO'd . . . In the *cooler* self-pity overcame me in the end, after all. It came in handy, as I knew that I would have to put on a distraught face later on, when the key scraped in the lock and they let me out; let them enjoy the presumed torment they had inflicted on me. (Did I know about these little tricks instinctively, out of an inborn cunning, or did I merely acquire them very early on, the fruits of *a successful education*?) . . . By that time I had long been wise to just how foul a place the world is for a young child (little did I know that this would not change later on unless I myself were to change) . . . And the headaches. One can't help remembering them. Migraines, to give them their proper name. That's what they were. I was unable to move, the throbbing from the light on my eyes. I never dared mention them to anybody. I didn't believe that I would be believed, that others could believe, that it was believable. I believed they too were just a sin that was my secret alone, and therefore to be kept secret like the other things, like everything else. In the end, I did not even believe my own head when it was aching. This, likewise an educational success . . . Just consider the chances of surviving the whole thing, from the age of five to the age of ten. Almost inconceivable: how? Obviously, like others, like everybody else, by dint of massive, irrational, sledgehammer blows to my rationality. By dint of madness, the madness that separates (or, for that matter, unites) slavish madness from domineering madness. The first irrational determinant: my father's and mother's divorce, which was of interest chiefly in that its consequence was the school. When I nagged them for a *reason* for their divorce, the answer, both my father's and my mother's, was always: *Because we didn't understand one another.* How could that be? Both of them speak Hungarian after all, I thought to myself. I just could not comprehend why they would *not* understand when they plainly did *understand* one another. But then that was the final word, the clinching argument, a blank wall: I therefore suspected that behind it lay some weighty complicated and presumably nasty secret that they were foisting on me. It bore a resemblance to a nemesis: I had to accept it and the more (because it was all the more a nemesis) the less I understood it. The second irrational determinant was a certain tram journey that I regularly took with my father. Where we went, to whom or why, I no longer recollect. The whole matter was a lot more insignificant than the divorce. All the same. The stop where we always got off and after that a long walk in the same direction as the tram. I ventured the remark that from the next stop we would only have to go back a few paces. The response was: *I don't go back.* Question: *Why?* Answer: *Because I don't go back.* Question anew: *But why not?* Answer anew: *I've already told you: because I don't go back.* I sensed the enormous profundity of this obduracy, only I could not puzzle it out. Total, crushing perplexity of my intellect, as if faced with some revealed secret. In the end, all I was able and indeed *had* to deduce was some inscrutable but incontestable principle that my father represented, and the power he wielded over me. "Neurosis and coercion as a system of exclusive types of relationship, accommodation as the sole possibility of surviving, obedience as drill, lunacy as final outcome," I wrote. *The earlier culture crumbles into a heap of rubble and finally a heap of ashes, but spirits will hover over the ashes*, that too is on one of my slips of paper (Wittgenstein), ". . . and as I was standing there, under my umbrella, and as I was brushed by the stifling secret of this establishment, this well-healed private institution, this former *State Lic. Boarding School*, a stifling secret which even today flutters about in the damp autumnal air, just as a malevolent silence bangs around the burial vaults of antiquity, all at once—how should I put it?—I was little short of pervaded by this *earlier culture*, this paternalistic-culture, this worldwide father-complex as by the all-pervading damp . . . ," I wrote. On coming across descriptions of private schools, seminaries and military colleges in the course of my subsequent reading, I occasionally fancied I recognized "my school," though of course that was different all the same, more genial, more absurd and, on the whole, even more perverse, though I was only able to recognize this fully, in the mirror of all-consummating shame, after many years had gone by, I said to my wife. In reality, it was based on simple principles, the principles of respect and authoritarian paternalism, I said to my wife. It simply replicated the principles of the outside world, and whether out of habit or comic miscalculation, or through habit that slid into comic miscalculation, it regarded those principles as its title to domination, I said to my wife. On the wall of the classrooms a picture of Hungary's father-usurper of the day: among the imperial and royal highnesses, secretary-generals and first secretaries of state, was a half-length portrait of the man honored as His Serene Highness the Regent, resplendent in his admiral's cap and baffling shoulder-tasseled uniform, I said to my wife. Thus, looking back on it, I said to my wife, I am beginning to suspect that the boarding school's administration may well have been influenced by Anglo-

Saxon administrative and Anglo-Saxon *educational* ideals, with some leavening of Austro-German, no, Austro-Hungarian, no, Germano-Austro-Hungarian-assimilated-Jewish-minority elements, by virtue of the *genius loci*; albeit, I said to my wife, with the difference that here they were not training the elite of a world empire, but members of Budapest's middle, lower middle and even lower bourgeoisie. Spartan principles were evident at most in the inadequate catering; under the influence of scholarly and Anglo-Saxon ideals, the school management *stole* the food from the boys, obviously by virtue of the same *genius loci*, I said to my wife. I also mentioned the commemorative plaque to my wife, and how greatly it had astonished me. If I wanted to, I said to my wife, I could undoubtedly find out more about it, the commemorative plaque, that is, the reason for it, and so on, but for my part I don't have any desire to know anything. True enough, that man, the headmaster and also proprietor of our school, was invested with immense authority, but that authority carried not the slightest trace of any esteem for higher things: as befits such authority, his too was based only on well-organized terror, I said to my wife, even though he himself was a rather ridiculous figure (at this point I mentioned the nickname that we boys gave him: Fat Nat), a diminutive man with a long, bushy, drooping, yellowish-white mustache, an artistically sweeping forelock of white hair, his paunch, almost a separate body part, swelling like a huge watermelon under his grey waistcoat. Otherwise, that's all there was to it; don't imagine anything more, I said to my wife, no brutal acts, no rough words to inspire our terror. But then terror, my dear, I said to my wife, operates by multiple transference, and by the time it becomes consolidated into a world order it is often little more than a superstition. The teachers feared him, or at least acted as if they feared him. He served as a fixed point of reference for them, his approach accompanied by whispering, hissing, a general snatching-up of things. The Head! The Head's coming! Only rarely did he come. His orders and messages, indeed often undeclared wishes that were merely attributed to, one could say anticipated from, him arrived from his apartment on the second floor like from a citadel on high. We lived under the badge of that citadel, our gazes constantly raised to it, eyes peeled but taking on a shifty look in its shadow. Solemnity reigned, the well foundedness no one doubted in the least, an oppressive solemnity that simultaneously bore a touch of official heartiness. A spirit of playing by the rules of the game and of sportsmanship, a spirit of the *seniors'* approaching examinations and graduation. A spirit of modernity, yet replete with classical traditions. Along with nationalistic curriculum, nationalistic declamations, nationalistic mourning, nationalistic avowals. I recall the legends, I related to my wife, that circulated among us about the dishes that were hauled from the kitchen in the basement up the back steps that led directly to the citadel; there was always someone around who just happened to have seen what they had carried up for the Head and his family's lunch or dinner while we picked at four slices of sausage, cut into a plate of watery, paprika-spiced potatoes, or at the five biscuits served with the suppertime mug of tea. But as we know all too well, my dear, I related to my wife, privilege only bolsters authority, and the awe tinged with hatred with which we subordinated beings perceived these demonstrations very much fitted in with the general ambiguity of our lives. Although, I related to my wife, the solemnity did sometimes collapse, creaking and groaning, and tumble into some abyss, ringed by obscene sniggering, from which the demented whooping of the resident demons would drift up on these occasions but out of which the old regime, the citadel, order, would always reemerge, battered maybe, like a battleship raised from the ocean bed, but triumphant even as a wreck. *Scandal*, I related to my wife, that's what they called these irresistible, always unexpected plunges into licentiousness, so to say, which you should imagine, I said to my wife, as somewhat like when an inebriated gentleman, having kept a strict hold on himself for a good while, suddenly yields to temptation and falls flat on the ground in relief, yes, these derailments were like that, with the added remark that the gentleman's sobriety itself is nothing other than a derailment and loss of footing, the sobriety merely a heightened inebriation, I said to my wife. I told her the story of one such scandal. One of the most characteristic ones. When that ass "Black Jack," an aging, heavy-handed tutor, stormed through the dormitories one morning to discover that one of us was missing, a *senior*, a seventeen-year-old boy whose white teeth, animated face, long brown hair and laugh I can call to mind even today, I said to my wife. At the same time (or it may have been earlier), he discovered that the small room which opened onto the end of the corridor could not be opened, that is to say, it was locked, and what was more, locked from the inside. At the same time (or it may have been earlier), the kitchen reported the "new girl" as missing, and I can still remember the girl as well, how she served at the tables in her housemaid's apron, though in truth all I can remember are her blonde curls and a rather typical, I might say archetypal, smile. Allegedly, they had locked themselves in the evening before then gone to sleep. "Black Jack" was now pounding on the door. After a hesitant rummaging and stifled whispering no further sounds could be heard on the outside. They did not open the door. "Black Jack" beseeched the culprits, and so on. Not long after, along came the Head. His face flushed, his mustache and forelock flouncing, his paunch wobbling up and down, with us malicious underlings flattening ourselves against the wall to let him through. He tugged at the handle like the Gestapo, hammered on the door with both fists like the cuckolded husband in a low farce. Then all I recollect is the public expulsion (the girl, of course, was kicked out instantly), the artful, unctuous and treacherous text, the fact that everyone of us took the side of the *senior*, and also every one of us remained silent. Only natural, you might say, I said to my wife. I now know the basis of my sense of guilt, my guilty conscience, my terror and my shame, the choking sensation that I felt during the whole procedure; I now know what sort of ritual it was that I witnessed in that paternalistic, father-usurping institution: I witnessed a *public castration* staged for purposes of our intimidation, *with our cooperation*; in other words, with our cooperation they castrated one of our pals *in order to intimidate us*, or in other words, through the very ceremony itself they turned us into the ultimately perverted accomplices of an ultimately perverted act, I said to my wife, and it makes not the slightest difference, I said to my wife, whether they did this quite deliberately or merely out of habit, out of sheer *educational habit*, the pernicious habit of a pernicious education. Or take, for instance, the *report* assembly every Saturday afternoon, I said to my wife. That, too, has to be pictured, I said to her. First of all, a number of long trestles were brought out of the dining hall and made into a single, endlessly long table, which they then covered. This was all staged in the games room. Only then were we pupils admitted, lining up to face this endlessly long, covered but empty table, not forgetting the row of chairs set up behind it. Anxiety would already be starting to weigh on us like some palpable substance. Then somebody, usually one of the lower-tutors, but it might be one of the higher-ranking members of the lower-ranking staff, brought in a large, black-bound book, the *report book*, and silently placed it in the middle of the table. A further period of waiting would ensue, a wait of ever-decreasing hopefulness in the face of the chairs, the table and that mute, evil, flat report book, sprawling in its blackness on the white tablecloth. At that moment, at the moment of all-around vacillation, sighs and, yes, total enervation, the *Headmaster* would enter at the head of the teaching staff. They would take their places. Deathly silence. A putting-on of spectacles. Some clearing of throats, creaking of chairs. And when the tension could be screwed no higher, the black book would be opened, like a Book of the Apocalypse. Everybody was in it, and everybody's every sin (and virtue). Each of us was individually addressed by name. On being called out, you would step forward and tremble alone in the space between the authorities ensconced behind the table and the warmth of the flock you had just forsaken. Keeping a rough idea of your merits and transgressions in mind, yet with growing uncertainty about even these, you would be prepared for any eventuality. The Head would silently read the week's entries about you, turn to the right, turn to the left, for a whispered consultation, with teachers bowing an ear or mouth towards him, and then the verdict would be pronounced. It might be a reprimand, praise or a tongue-lashing, you might be declared an example to the rest, or they might revoke your Saturday and even Sunday pass. But it wasn't that, it was the ceremony itself, the *procedure*, that was the essential thing, I said to my wife. I sensed that perhaps I should not be telling my wife all these things, at least not this way, speaking about nothing else for days and weeks on end, because it was likely that I was boring her, and quite certain that I was tormenting her with this, just as I was only tormenting myself too, albeit much less than her, of course; or to be more accurate, I tormented myself not just less but also differently, more productively, one might say, than I tormented her, and I already sensed this at the time, while I was talking, while I was telling my wife about my childhood, already then as I was talking I distinctly sensed a continual building-up, swelling and tensing within me of the long-gone carbuncle of my childhood, now suddenly reinflamed by a new threat and looking to rupture, indeed rupturing, so by talking I was admittedly tormenting myself, but at the same time I also found relief through talking, through this torment. The ceremony, I said to my wife, was just like a religious service, the way a corporal, let's say, might imagine it, I said to my wife; yes, the ceremony was like an *Appell* at Auschwitz, not for real, of course, just in fun, I said to my wife. I learned later that the Head, too, had gone up in smoke in one of the crematoria there, and if I cannot help perceiving this fact as an ultimate justification, so to speak, then most probably that is still a fruit of the successful education acquired from him, of the *culture* in which he believed and for which he equipped me pedagogically, I said to my wife. Out of this, after all, essentially cooler, more impersonal and thus actually more predictable world of pedagogical dictatorship, I then suddenly came under a warmhearted paternal rule of terror, for when I was ten my father took me back home, I told my wife. Around this time, I recollect, I made several attempts to set down in writing a picture of my father and my feelings towards my father, of the—what can I say?—fairly complicated relationship between my father and myself, an at least somewhat accurate, although of course not entirely true—because how could one be true towards one's father? how indeed could I be true even towards the truth itself? since for me there exists only one truth, *my own truth*, and even if that is a mistake, yes, my life alone, God help us!, only my own life can vouchsafe my own mistake as the sole truth—so anyway, I tried to create at least some sort of acceptable portrait, as I said, of my father and my feelings towards my father and my relationship with him, but this never succeeded, and now I know that it can never succeed, and I also as good as know, or anyway I have an idea, or at least an inkling, that I have been constantly trying to do exactly this ever since, and when all is said and done that is all I am doing right now, and, now as ever, doing it in vain. "I have to become capable of realizing how impossible it was for him to find the path to me . . ." I wrote, for instance . . . "Plainly, he was bound by a tense relationship to me as to himself, which he plainly called love, and believed to be that, which indeed it was, if we are ready to accept the word in all its absurdity and disregard its tyrannical content . . ." I wrote. At the school I had had dealings with a law, and though I may have feared it, I never had any respect for it, I said to my wife. In point of fact, it bore an aspect of fortune: it might come down hard on me or in my favor, but in neither case did it touch my conscience; only under the yoke of love did I become a real sinner, I said to my wife. This phase of my childhood pitched me into an unimaginably narrow-minded crisis; I lived in an animistic belief-world, like a caveman, my thoughts hedged about by so many taboos that I ascribed almost material powers to them, believing in their omnipotence, I said to my wife. Meanwhile, however, and undoubtedly under my father's influence, I also supposed there was an Almighty who would know my every thought at the moment of its inception and weigh it in the balance, but then I was often assailed by imponderable thoughts. It was one of my father's habits, for instance, to appeal to my better nature from time to time, I said to my wife. On such occasions, he found it impossible to avoid repeating himself; in other words, I said to my wife, I always knew what he was going to say next, secretly I was always ahead of him in the text that, like a catechism, he obligingly repeated after me: for a moment I would regain my freedom, though it also made my flesh creep, I said to my wife. Terror-stricken, I would try to cling on to something; it would be enough to notice his hapless, dog-eared shirt collar, the loneliness of his slightly trembling hand, the strained furrowing of his brow, his quite futile torment—anything to unnerve me and make me pervious as a desiccated sponge. Then at last I could inwardly intone the redemptive words, the words of brief triumph and at the same time hasty retreat: *Poor thing* . . . The sponge would begin to swell, I would be moved to tears by my own emotions, and I thereby paid off some of the debt that continually weighed on me as a result of my father's intimidating love. As to whether, when all is said and done, despite everything, and mindful of all the ambiguities of the word, I really loved him, I answered my wife, who put the question to me at this point, I don't know; indeed, it would be exceedingly difficult for me to know, because, faced with so many reproaches and so many demands, I always knew and felt and saw, or I *ought* to have known, felt and seen, that I didn't love him, or at least did not love him properly, not *enough*, and therefore, because I was *unable* to love him, I indeed probably did not love him, I said to my wife; and in my opinion, I said to my wife, that was also as it should be, putting it somewhat radically, the way it was planned, I said to my wife, for that way, and only that way, we were able to produce an *ideally routinized structure of existence.* Domination is unchallengeable, unchallengeable the laws by which we must live, though we can never fully live up to these laws: we are always sinners before our father and God, I said to my wife. After all, my father likewise only equipped me for the same thing, the same *culture*, as the school, and he probably gave as little thought to his goals as I to my reluctance, my disobediences, my failures: we may not have understood one another, but our cooperation worked perfectly, I said to my wife. And even if I have no idea whether I loved him or not, the fact is there were many times when I honestly pitied him, with all my heart: but if, by sometimes making him ridiculous, and pitying him because of that, if by doing that—in secret, always in the greatest secrecy—I thereby overthrew paternal power, respect, God, it was not just that he—my father—lost his authority over me, but I myself became achingly lonely, I said to my wife. I had need of a tyrant for my world order to be restored, I said to my wife, but my father never tried to replace my usurpatory world order with another, one based on our common state of powerlessness, for example, in other words, one based on truth, I said to my wife. And in the same way, just as I was a bad son and bad pupil, so I was also a bad Jew, I said to my wife. My Jewishness remained an obscure circumstance of birth, just one of my many faults, a bald-headed woman in a red negligee in front of the mirror, I said to my wife. Of course, I said many other things too to my wife, I no longer recall them all. I do remember that I exhausted her very much, just as I became very tired myself and am still tired now. Later on, Auschwitz, I said to my wife, seemed to me to be just an exaggeration of the very same virtues to which I had been educated since early childhood. Yes, childhood and education were the start of that inexcusable process of breaking me, the survival that I never survived, I said to my wife. Even if my progress was not always with top marks, I was a modestly diligent party to the silent conspiracy that was woven against my life, I said to my wife. Auschwitz, I said to my wife, manifests itself to me in the image of a father; yes, the words father and Auschwitz elicit the same echo within me, I said to my wife. And if the assertion that God is a glorified father figure holds any truth, then God manifested himself to me in the image of Auschwitz, I said to my wife. When I finally fell silent, and after all the talking I stayed silent for a long while, perhaps days, my wife seemed to be in torment, but it was as if she had not grasped what I had been saying, or to be more precise, as if she had not grasped what I had been saying in the way that I said it, that is, as if she had not noticed that I, without any reason (to say the least of it)—and it was useless my being aware of it, of course—but without any reason, mercilessly, and in all likelihood merely because she had heard me out, I had in fact directed all my anger at her, and to avoid having to use the word revolt here, in this connection, where it truly has no place, what I am saying is that it was as if my wife perhaps supposed that now I had related all this, given vent to it, vomited it out of myself, I had in the process *freed myself* from it all; yes, as if I could have freed myself from all this, as if it were ever possible to free myself from it all—that may have been what she supposed, I supposed, noticing several, admittedly tentative attempts on her part to draw closer, to draw closer to me *by understanding*. By nature I closed myself off from that; by nature I was unable to bear any sort of *understanding*, for in reality that would only have served to sanction my powerlessness. But that was as nothing compared with the elemental force of the insight that probably sprang purely from *my procedure*, from the way that I treated my wife, or yes, in the final hours of my glittering night I ought to use the appropriate word for it, because it is the only cathartic word: so, from the way that I disposed of her. Yes, my being so merciless, so *intimately merciless*, towards her had, in the process, made her, it seemed, once and for all unacceptable in my eyes; in a certain sense, and what I am about to say is an exaggeration, of course, a big exaggeration, but in a certain sense it was as if I had killed her, which made her a witness to it, she had looked on, she would have seen me killing a person; and it seemed that I would never be able to forgive her for that. It is superfluous for me to reflect on that period here; for instance, on how much longer we lived, were able to live, like that, mutely alongside one another. I was deeply depressed, inert and lonely, this time to a degree that it proved impossible to compensate for; in other words, it did not bring *my work* any further forward, on the contrary, it totally paralyzed it. I am not absolutely sure if, while I was inwardly—naturally—in the very process of fabricating accusations, a whole web of accusations, against her, I was not secretly waiting for help from my wife; but even if this was the case, I gave no visible sign of it, in my opinion. One day, in the evening if I recall correctly, and late in the evening at that, my wife had just arrived home from somewhere, I don't know where, I didn't pry, I didn't even ask where, she was looking beautiful, and just for a passing moment, like a flash of lightning behind thick clouds, the thought briefly cleaved through me: "What a pretty Jewish girl!" naturally, shamelessly and sadly, as she entered, and it seemed that she was traversing a greenish-blue carpet as if she were making her way on the sea, and it was then, that night, that she, my wife, broke the silence, our silence. It was somewhat late, my wife said, but she could see I was still up, sitting and reading. She was sorry, my wife said, but some business had come up, though that was probably of no interest to me anyway. That I was sitting there and reading, reading or writing, reading *and* writing, it was all the same, my wife said. Yes, my wife said, it had been a great lesson for her, the whole thing, our marriage, that is to say. Through me, my wife said, she had come to understand and experience everything that she had not understood, and had not wanted to understand either, based on her own parents' experiences. No, because to have understood everything, she knew now, would then, when she was a young girl, simply have killed her. Secretly, my wife said, in the depths of her soul, she had believed she was a coward, but now she knew—and I, along with the years spent with me, had helped her significantly in this—well, now she knew that she had simply wanted to live, had to live. And now also, my wife said, now also that was what everything within her was saying, she wanted to live. She was sorry for me and, above all, sorry that she was so powerless in feeling sorry for me; but then she had done everything within her power *to save me* (I kept quiet, but her choice of words surprised me). Even if purely out of gratitude, my wife continued, for I had shown her the way, though it was me, of all people, who had subsequently been unable to keep up with her along it, because the wounds that I carried within me, and from which I might, perhaps, have been able to recover but, it seemed—or at least so it seemed to her, my wife said—I had not *wanted*, and still did not want, to recover from, were tougher than my mind, and that had carried over into our love and our marriage. She said again that she was sorry for me, she said others had destroyed me, but I had also destroyed myself in the process, though that had not been the way she had viewed it at first, on the contrary, at first *what she had admired in me* was that, while others might have tried to destroy me, I had nevertheless not been destroyed, as she had seen it then; she had been wrong about that, my wife said, but that would not have been a problem in itself, and it had not given rise to a sense of disappointment, though she had undoubtedly suffered on that account, my wife said. She repeated that she had wanted to save me, but the fruitlessness of all her attempts, her affection and her love had slowly killed any love and affection she had towards me and had left her just with a sense of fruitlessness and futility and unhappiness. She said that I had always talked a lot about freedom, but the freedom to which I was constantly in the habit of referring did not, for me, in reality, signify freedom in my vocation as an *artist* (as my wife put it), indeed in reality was not freedom at all, if by freedom one means expansive, strong, receptive, to which commitment, yes, *love* can also be added, my wife said; no, my kind of freedom was, in effect, a freedom directed *against* something or somebody, and somebodies or somethings, my wife said, fight or flight, or both together, and without that my kind of freedom did not actually even exist, because—it would appear—it could not exist, my wife said. And so, if these "somebodies or somethings" were not to hand, then I invent and create dependencies of that sort, my wife said, in order that there be something for me to flee from or confront. And I had thereby, for years now, mercilessly and cunningly allotted to her this appalling—or, to be honest just for once: this *shameful*—role (to use one of my own expressions), my wife said, but not in the manner a lover seeking support would use to his lover, nor even a patient to his doctor; no, my wife said, I had allotted this role to her (to use one of my favorite words again) like a hangman to his victim, my wife said. She said that I had bowled her over with my mind, then aroused her sympathy, then having aroused her sympathy, had made her my audience, an audience for my appalling childhood and my horrific stories, and when she had wanted to have a part in these stories, in order to steer the stories out of their maze, their rut, yes, their mire, and guide me to her, to her love, so that *together* we might extricate ourselves from the swamp and leave it behind forever, like the bad memory of an illness—then all at once I had let go of her hand (as my wife expressed it) and started to run away from her, back into the swamp, and now she no longer had the strength, my wife said, to come after me a second time, and who knows how many times more, to lead me out of there again. Because it seemed, my wife said, that I don't even want to make a start on fumbling my way out of there; evidently, for me there was no way out of my appalling childhood and horrific stories, whatever she might do, my wife said, and even if she were to sacrifice her life for me, she knew, she saw, that she would be doing it only fruitlessly, to no avail. Yes, when we had bumped into one another (that was the phrase my wife used), it had seemed to her that I might teach her how *to live*, and then she had been horrified to see how much destructive force I had within me, and that next to me what was in store for her was not life but destruction. The cause, my wife said, was a sick intellect, a sick and poisoned intellect, she repeated over and over again, an eternally poisoned and poisoning and contaminating intellect which, my wife said, had to be brought to an end; yes, my wife said, one just had to free oneself, detach oneself, from it, if one wanted to live, and she had decided, she repeated, that she wanted to live. At this juncture my wife fell silent for a moment, and from the way she stood there, her shoulders slightly hunched, arms folded, lonely, alarmed, pale faced, her lipstick smudged, I was suddenly—or, let's say, unavoidably—struck by a solicitous concern that maybe she was feeling cold. And then, swiftly and drily, as if it were some unpleasant news that would, however, immediately lose its unpleasant flavor as soon as she was able to announce it, she went on to say that, yes, there was no point in hiding it, there "was someone," someone whom she was thinking of marrying. And *he*, she added, was not Jewish. It is interesting, perhaps, that it was only now that I spoke up, as if out of all that my wife had said I felt aggrieved by just this one point. What did she take me for, some sort of negative race preservationist? I bawled at her. I didn't need to have been in Auschwitz, I bawled, to learn about this age and this world, and not deny any longer what I have learned, I bawled, not to deny it in the name of some curious—albeit, I admit it, exceedingly practical—interpretation of the principle of life, which is actually just the principle of accommodation; all right, I bawled, I have no objections to it, but let us see clearly, I bawled, let us see clearly that *assimilation* in this instance is not the assimilation of one race—race! don't make me laugh!—to another race—don't make me laugh!—but a *total assimilation* to the extant, the extant circumstances and existing conditions, I bawled, circumstances and conditions which may be such or such, it's not worth ranking them according to their qualities—they are the way they are—the only thing that is worth ranking, but then it is *our bounden duty* to rank it, is our *decision*, our decision to carry out total assimilation, or not to carry out total assimilation, I bawled, though probably more quietly by this point, and then we should, indeed it is *our bounden duty* to, rank our capabilities as to whether or not we are able to carry out total assimilation; and already in early childhood I could see clearly that I was incapable of it, incapable of assimilating to the extant, the existing, *to life*, and despite that, I bawled, I am nevertheless extant, I exist and I live, but in such a way that I know I am incapable of it, in such a way that already in early childhood I could see clearly that if I were to assimilate, that would kill me sooner than if I did not assimilate, which actually would likewise kill me anyway. And in this respect it is absolutely irrelevant whether I am a Jew or not a Jew, though Jewishness is, undeniably, a great advantage here, and from this perspective—do you understand? I bawled—*from this* unique *perspective alone* am I willing to be Jewish, exclusively from this unique perspective do I regard it as fortunate, even especially fortunate, indeed a blessing, not to be a Jew, because I don't care a hoot, I bawled, what I am, but to have had the opportunity of being in Auschwitz as a branded

Jew and yet, through my Jewishness, to have lived through something and confronted something; and I know, once and for all, and I know irrevocably something that I will not relinquish, will never relinquish, I bawled. I soon fell silent. After that we divorced. And if I do not recall the years that succeeded this as years in the desert of total barrenness, that is purely thanks to the fact that during these years, as always—since then, before then and naturally during the period of my marriage as well—*I worked*; yes, it was my work that saved me, even if in reality, of course, it has only saved me for destruction. During those years I not only arrived at certain decisive intuitions, during these years I became aware that my intuitions were in turn tightly interwoven, knot to knot, with my destiny. During those years I also became aware of the true nature of my work, which in essence is nothing other than to dig, dig further and to the end, the grave that others started to dig for me in the clouds, the winds, the nothingness. During those years I dreamed anew the task and secret hope that had been dreamed before, and now I know it was a dream based on "Teacher's" example. During these years I became aware of my life, on the one hand as fact, on the other as a *cerebral mode of existence*, to be more precise, a certain mode of existence that would no longer survive, did not wish to survive, indeed probably was not even capable of surviving survival, a life which nevertheless has its own demand, namely, that it *be formed*, like a rounded, rock-hard object, in order that it should *persist*, after all, no matter why, no matter for whom—*for everybody and nobody*, for whoever it is or isn't, it's all the same, for whoever will feel shame on our account and (possibly) for us; which I shall put an end to and liquidate, however, as *fact*, as the mere fact of survival, even if, and truly only if, that fact happens to be me. During those years it happened that I came across Dr. Obláth in the woods. During those years I started to write my slips of paper about my marriage. During those years my wife looked me up again. Once when I was waiting in the usual coffee house, hoping for more prescriptions, she led in two children by the hand. One was a dark-eyed little girl with pale spots of freckles scattered around her tiny nose, one a headstrong boy with eyes bright and hard as greyish-blue pebbles. *Say hello to the gentleman*, she told them. That sobered me up completely, once and for all. Sometimes I still scurry through the city like a bedraggled weasel that has managed to make it through a big extermination drive. I start at each sound or sight, as if the scent of faltering memories were assailing my calloused, sluggish senses from the other world. Here and there, by a house or street corner, I stop in terror, I search around with alarmed looks, nostrils flaring, I want to flee but something holds me back. Beneath my feet the sewers bubble, as if the polluted flood of my memories were seeking to burst out of its hidden channel and sweep me away. Let it; I am ready for it. In one last big effort to regain my composure, I have produced my still fallible, stubborn life—I have produced it so that I may set off with the bundle that is this life in my two upraised arms and, for all I care, in the swirling black waters of some dark river,

May I submerge,
Lord God!
let me submerge
for ever and ever,
Amen.